Manolito Four-Eyes

The 2nd Volume of
the Great Encyclopedia of My Life

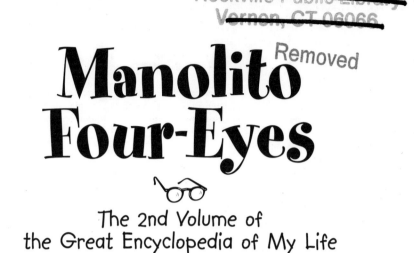

Manolito Four-Eyes

The 2nd Volume of
the Great Encyclopedia of My Life

BY ELVIRA LINDO

ILLUSTRATED BY EMILIO URBERUAGA

TRANSLATED BY CAROLINE TRAVALIA

MARSHALL CAVENDISH CHILDREN

Marshall Cavendish Corporation
99 White Plains Road
Tarrytown, NY 10591
www.marshallcavendish.us/kids

Library of Congress Cataloging-in-Publication Data
Lindo, Elvira
[Pobre Manolito. English]
The 2nd volume of the great encyclopedia of my life / by Elvira Lindo ; illustrated by Emilio Urberuaga ; translated by Caroline Travalia.
p. cm. — (Manolito Four-Eyes)
Summary: Ten-year-old Manolito recounts further exploits in his small Madrid neighborhood with his grandfather, his little brother, the Bozo, and his school friends, including a shoplifting prank, recycled art, and the Filthy Feet Gang.
ISBN 978-0-7614-5470-0
[1. Family life—Spain—Fiction. 2. Grandfathers—Fiction. 3. Schools—Fiction. 4. Spain—Fiction.] I. Urberuaga, Emilio, ill. II. Title. III. Title: Second volume of the great encyclopedia of my life. IV. Series.
PZ7.L65911Aac 2009
[Fic]—dc22
2008006481

Book design by Jay Colvin
Editor: Robin Benjamin

Printed in China
First Marshall Cavendish edition, 2009
10 9 8 7 6 5 4 3 2 1

mc Marshall Cavendish
Children

This book is dedicated to my dearest son Miguel, for all the ideas he has given me for these stories. And to my niece Patricia, who time and again has expressed her enthusiasm for Manolito Four-Eyes. To both of them, because they, like Manolito, are full of happiness and tenderness. May this book always help them to remember these years when they are still children.

CAST OF CHARACTERS

Manolito Four-Eyes
A ten-year-old boy from
Carabanchel, he's a chatterbox
who's misunderstood.

Grandpa Nicolás
Manolito's unconditional ally

The Bozo
Manolito's favorite little
brother—he only has one!

The One-and-Only Susana

This girl is like a whirlwind. Her limitless imagination can get anyone in trouble, especially Manolito.

Ozzy

The biggest bully and troublemaker in Manolito's school

Big Ears

A despicable traitor and Manolito's inseparable friend

Miss Asunción

Even though she thinks all her students are delinquents, she never loses hope that they'll change.

Manolito Four-Eyes

The 2nd Volume of
the Great Encyclopedia of My Life

1

This Is Only the Beginning

I'm back. It's me again, Manolito, the same guy from the first book called *Manolito Four-Eyes*. Some people like to think they know everything about my life just because they read that book. There are people on planet Earth that think they're really smart. My grandpa Nicolás says you could fill up encyclopedias with my life; and he's not just saying that because he's my grandpa, he's saying it because it's true. In the ten years I've been living on the ball of the world (the worldwide world), so many things have happened that even if I spent the next ninety years telling them all, I wouldn't finish. I say ninety because, if I had my choice, I'd like to die when I'm one hundred. Dying

3

before that just isn't worth it. That's what I tell my grandpa: "Dying at eighty-seven isn't cool, Grandpa; you gotta die at one hundred, like a king, with two fat zeros like donuts."

I don't get how some really important people go to write their memoirs when they're old and they only write like 357 pages. I'm telling you: I'm only ten, but I couldn't fit my life in 357 pages. So I'll have to keep writing book after book after book so that you can find out the truth about my life: *Manolito Gets a New Sweatsuit*, *The Bozo Has a Name*, *Manolito's Jokes*, *Manolito in New York*. Well, the last one's science fiction, because I'm never going to be in New York. It's a family tradition, not going to New York. It's almost as old as the Spanish tradition of eating twelve grapes at the stroke of midnight on New Year's Eve or dancing the conga at Carabanchel parties. As far as I know, none of my ancestors ever went to New York, and I don't think I'm going to be the first, because in the ten years I've been on planet Earth I haven't been the first at anything; just ask Miss Asunción, who defined me at the end of last year as "your classic ordinary kid." But I don't want to give away the end of the book. I'm not gonna be like Big Ears López, who goes to see a movie three days before you do so he can tell you the end and ruin it for you. That's just the sort of thing my dear friend (even though he's a dirty traitor) gets a kick out of.

This book is about the adventures I've had in the past few months, and there are so many things that happen to me every day that it was hard to decide which stories to tell. And, to make matters worse, everyone I know had to put in their two cents.

Ozzy told me that if I didn't put in the adventure about the whistle we'd have a showdown at high noon in Hangman's Park.

The One-and-Only Susana asked me to make all the chapters about her ". . . and not like in the last book where you only told about my underwear, wise guy," she said.

Our Nosy Neighbor Luisa didn't want me to include the story about the piggies, but since deep down she thought it was funny, she proposed that she and her husband, Bernabé (who is also my godfather), appear under pseudonyms. In the end, I forgot and used their real names instead. My mom said, "I can't wait to see the consequences of your little book in the neighborhood."

The Bozo, my little brother, who for the moment is illiterate, only has one obsession: he wants to be in all the illustrations. So he'll grab the book and point with his pacifier at the illustrations he's in (getting slobber all over the pages) and say, "Me."

And he'll turn the pages till he finds himself again. When he knows how to read, he's going to insist on being the main character. I guarantee it.

Arturo Román's mom called my mom to say, "My Arturo is such a good friend of Manolito's. I can't believe the poor guy only had two lines last time."

Big Ears confessed the other day that, after giving it a

lot of thought, he had come to the conclusion that the coolest parts are the ones he's in.

"I'm telling you from the heart," he said, putting his hand on the right side of his chest (human anatomy isn't his strong point).

The owner of Stumbles Bar asked me not to mention that last year half of Carabanchel got food poisoning from one of his potato salads that had gone bad; so I'll keep that chapter to blackmail him from time to time.

The only ones who didn't protest and didn't ask me for anything are my dad (even though I know he's happy because he's in this book a ton) and my grandpa, who seeing that everyone was giving me a hard time said, "You do your own thing, Manolito. If they want to be in a book, they can write one themselves."

So that's what I did. I did my own thing; that's why I'm the one telling these terrifying stories.

Oh, before I forget: I want to thank Paquito Medina, who corrected all my spelling mistakes. Miss Asunción offered to correct them, but I didn't want her constantly reminding me what a big dunce I am. Plus, if I gave her the book, I'm sure she'd go and change it and turn it into *The Little Mermaid.* I know Paquito Medina will never tell that he had to correct 325 mistakes.

So here's the 2nd volume of the great encyclopedia of my life. Make room on the shelf because this is only the beginning.

2

The Good, the Bad and the Ugly

Boy, did I get chewed out the other day. My legs are still shaking from it. And I didn't just get chewed out; I got the worst punishment in the history of rock and roll. When my mom was yelling at me, telling me all the different things I was going to suffer through over the weekend, I said: "Could you please go a little slower? I wanna write this down."

So my mom started yelling even louder: "On top of it all, now you're trying to be cute, huh?"

That's how she is, all tough. I wrote down my punishment on a piece of paper and told my grandpa to make copies of it and put them up in strategic locations all over the apartment, those places I visit frequently: the toilet, the fridge, the TV, the sofa. I couldn't risk forgetting any of it. The repercussions would be terrible (you don't know my mom).

My punishment was as follows:

1. You will not watch TV all weekend. And you will not keep asking, "So, what can I do?"
2. You will not call the Bozo "The Bozo." And you will not keep asking, "Can someone tell me what his name is?"
3. You will not go to Hangman's Park with your friends.
4. You will not receive an allowance for two weeks.
5. You will eat your vegetables without saying, "This is gross."
6. You will help set and clear the table.
7. You will not hide Grandpa's dentures.
8. You will not ask for a reward for finding Grandpa's dentures.
9. You will wash your feet every night.
10. You will not eat cookies until further notice.

When my grandpa read these new commandments, he whispered to me, so that my mom couldn't hear: "Manolito, I think jail would have been better than this."

Jail . . . man, I really did come close to going to jail, the kind of jail that Our Teach, Miss Asunción, says there should be for kids like us who are troublemakers.

I wish I had a guardian angel, like the ones Our Nosy Neighbor Luisa says kids used to have to keep them out of

trouble during their lives. Luisa says that years ago, every kid had an invisible guardian angel at his side and that, for example, the kid would be walking down the street and a car'd almost hit him, but the guardian angel would make the car crash into a tree at the last fatal second so that the kid could keep walking along his merry way in the middle of the road. And that, for another example, the kid would be in the country and there'd be this humongous storm and this killer bolt of lightning would be about to strike the kid from behind; but then a kind farmer would put himself between the lightning bolt and the kid, and while the farmer would be agonizing in pain on the ground, the kid would keep walking without even knowing what had happened behind him. And all thanks to the work of the guardian angel who, with a kid like that, must have always been on the verge of a heart attack.

The guardian angel was kind of like Superman, but instead of a cape he had wings because . . . well, after all, he *was* an angel! But nowadays, this angel just isn't used anymore; he's an out-of-style angel. At least for me, no guardian angel has ever watched my back, or any other kid's back in Carabanchel, and I could certainly use some help because I'm an expert at getting into trouble.

Man, I wish a guardian angel would've warned me not to pay attention to tough-guy Ozzy. He would've saved me from the mess I got into. I'll start my terrifying story from the beginning of time. . . .

Manolito Four-Eyes

The other day Big Ears and I were playing with a dung beetle we found in Hangman's Park when Ozzy, the bully of the neighborhood, showed up and went: "While you two sissies were playing with a beetle, I was stealing at Ms. Porfiria's store."

Ms. Porfiria's store is the most famous store in Carabanchel. Its specialties are expired yogurt and rancid lunch meat. I recommend you come one day to try them. In my family, we can't imagine life without these delicacies.

But back to what I was saying; Ozzy said he'd been stealing, and to prove it, the guy took out of his pockets gum, candy, melt-in-your-mouth-not-in-your-hand M&M's, and cookies. He also said he'd realized that stealing was sooo easy and that he was never going to pay for anything in a store again until he was old enough to have a Visa card. He said paying with a credit card was cool, but paying cash was so 80s.

That's what he said, those exact words. Big Ears and I were listening with our mouths wide open. I knew from my grandpa that you should not steal or cause harm to humanity, but then suddenly a guy comes along that has everything figured out and, c'mon, a kid isn't made of stone.

So, our killer gang decided to meet the next day, same time, same place: HANGMAN'S PARK, 5 PM

And why, you might ask, at 5 p.m. instead of 6 p.m.? Because that's when all the kids in my neighborhood get out of school and swarm Ms. Porfiria's store. According to my mother, Ms. Porfiria's gotta be a millionaire by now, with all the crap we buy from her.

Our plan was to take advantage of the store crawling with kids in order to carry out our attack.

The next day—H day (*H* for heist), T minus fifteen minutes (fifteen minutes before the agreed time)—all three of us were already under the lamppost in Hangman's Park ready to give the finishing touches to Plan P (*P* for Porfiria). The truth is that we really didn't look much like heisters. It's not easy to go from being a fantastic kid to a dangerous delinquent. We turned up the collars on our jackets to give us kind of a savage look.

"We coulda taken stockings from our moms and put 'em over our heads and that way nobody woulda recognized us!" yelled Big Ears on the way to the store.

"That woulda been cool," I said, imagining myself with the stocking smushing my nose.

"You know what people would say if they saw you guys with stockings over your faces?" Ozzy asked us. "They'd be like: 'There go Four-Eyes and Big Ears with stockings over their faces.'"

Ozzy has a special way of making you see in a second that your great ideas are really stupid.

The moment of truth had arrived. We were in front of Ms. Porfiria's store, on H day, ready to carry out Plan P at T minus one minute and counting. We looked at our watches to check if they were synchronized. Big Ears' watch

said midnight. What an idiot!

"It . . . stopped running a while ago," he tried to explain.

"So throw it out," said Ozzy, with no sympathy whatsoever.

"Well, my parents gave it to me when they got divorced, and I'm attached to it."

"Maybe he could just carry it in his pocket?" I said, trying to find a solution.

"All right, this time I'll let it slide," Ozzy said to Big Ears, and then he whispered to me, "Your little friend here is just causing problems, and we can't have that. A gang needs to be serious."

I waited for Ozzy to go into the store and then went up to Big Ears and said:

"Dude, you're just causing problems. A gang needs to be serious."

We followed him inside and got to work, stuffing our pockets with anything we could grab. Ozzy was right: it was so easy, we started laughing. We couldn't fit anything else in our pockets so we filled our underwear with gummy worms, marshmallows, and push-pops. All of a sudden, Ms. Porfiria stared at us and said, "What do you guys want?"

And Ozzy went: "We want one piece of gum for the three of us."

Man, you can't imagine how funny we thought Ozzy's answer was. We almost peed our pants from laughing so hard and from being so nervous. Luckily we didn't pee, because we were carrying part of the loot in our underwear.

Ms. Porfiria asked us where we were going to chew the gum, and we said Hangman's Park. And it was true. Telling the truth after committing a crime always feels good. She asked if we wanted her to split it exactly three ways, and that made us laugh again and we almost peed our pants a second time.

On the way to Hangman's Park, Ozzy said we were a three-man gang, like in a movie about cowboys he had seen, called *The Good, the Bad and the Ugly*. Big Ears and I started arguing because we both wanted to be the Good one, but Ozzy cleared that up pretty quick:

"No way. I'm the Good one, Big Ears is the Ugly one, and Manolito the Bad one."

Ozzy is an expert at putting a stop to any argument: he's right and that's all there is to it. When we got to Hangman's Park, we put our loot on the bench. There it was: everything you could imagine, the best banquet of our lives. We were about to pull down our pants to take out the rest when Big Ears pointed to a spot in the distance. Three dangerous-looking women were coming toward us. They were walking all bowlegged, as if they had each just gotten off a horse. It was useless to run away—those women were our mothers. There was no escape. A furious mother will find you anywhere. While they were coming closer, a little bit of wind picked up, and one of those tumbleweeds that always appear in cowboy movies when someone is about to get killed rolled by on the ground. And someone was definitely about to get killed. Finally, the tree in Hangman's Park was going to be put to use. The execution would be public. It was clear they had found out about our prank, but how could they have found out? You're probably wondering the same thing at this very moment.

Life is really something. A minute before I was peeing in my pants from laughing so hard, and now I was peeing in my pants from being so scared.

Big Ears' mom took him away without saying a word. Since she's divorced and feels guilty, she never yells at him. Ozzy started running toward his house, and his mom ran after him. Since he's a problem child, the only one who can really yell at him is the school psychologist. My mother doesn't beat around the bush and follows conventional, time-honored methods. She's a big fan of traditions. She chewed me out all the way to our front door.

I learned that they found out because Ms. Porfiria had been watching us all along, but she acted with the cold, calculated vengeance typical of storeowners. What a snitch!

Right now I'm pretty much a reformed kid. I will never steal again even if my kids don't have anything to eat. My grandpa says this has taught me a lesson, that I am so traumatized I won't ever steal again.

Our moms gave back all our loot to Ms. Porfiria, but . . . I had my secret stash: the stuff in my underwear.

Man, was it hard to peel off the candy. It was stuck all over. In the bathroom, I slowly peeled it off. Seriously, you can't imagine how much it hurt. It reminded me of when my mom waxes her legs. I washed it all off, wrapped it in my grandpa's scarf, and hid it under my pillow.

I've still got some left. Every night, when everyone's snoring, I take out my treasure, which is getting smaller and smaller, and I eat some before falling asleep. I know I shouldn't eat anything I stole, especially since I'm a reformed kid now, but tell me the truth, what would you do?

A Deadly Mistake

In this life, I have no choice but to be a fan of the Madrid soccer team, Real Madrid. My dad is a fan of Real; my uncle Nicolás (who's a waiter in Norway) is a fan of Real; everyone who shares my same genes is a fan of Real. Before there was Real Madrid—in caveman times—my ancestors, the first García Morenos that lived on this earth, came out of their cave one day, and admiring a typical prehistoric sunset, exclaimed:

"One day there will be soccer and a team called Real Madrid. We won't be there to see it."

"But our descendents will!"

What a moving scene! The thing is, if you live in Carabanchel and you're not a fan of Real, you better keep quiet or go somewhere else to live. If I weren't a fan of Real I'd be the disgrace of the family, Ozzy the Bully would beat me up, my dad wouldn't be able to walk down the street with his head held high, and Our Nosy Neighbor Luisa would say to my mom, "Your kid's not a fan of Real? Have you talked to the school psychologist about this?"

And don't think I'm exaggerating. I'll begin this story from the beginning of time: the seventh of January of this year.

✑

That historic Saturday, Real Madrid was playing a match against the Barcelona team, Barça, so my mom made two *tortillas de patata* (omelettes with fried potatoes), one underdone for my grandpa and my dad, who like the egg kind of snotty, and one for the Bozo and me, because we like ours drier than a raisin. She put everything in a picnic basket she bought on the Home Shopping Network and said good-bye to us with tears in her eyes.

We weren't the only ones going to see the match; we ran into a whole pilgrimage on the street, hundreds of thousands of people. We weren't headed to the soccer stadium, Santiago Bernabeu; no, we were headed to Stumbles, which is the most famous bar and café in my neighborhood.

Every time there's a soccer match, all the customers at Stumbles bring their lunch from home, because the owner says that on those historic days he's not about to be anybody's maid; and he's not gonna get up every two seconds, because that's how he's missed all the important goals in his lifetime. So his strategy is the following: before the game starts, he goes and asks all the dads, "How many cups of coffee are you going to have?" or "How many beers?" and if the dad tells him seventeen, for example, the owner says that doesn't seem like enough, that he better think long and hard about it before it's too late, and the dad goes, "All right, give me three more, better too many than too few." And after reaching this agreement, the owner of

Stumbles lines up the coffees in front of him and that's it. I've seen people crying in the middle of a game, begging him, "Mr. Ezequiel, give me another one, please. I ran out!"

And he's there behind the bar, totally unfazed, going, "Hey, too bad, buddy, you should have thought about that before the game started."

You won't believe it, but this setup goes over well. No dad has ever changed to another café. Mr. Ezequiel's slogan is, "The owner's always right. That's why he's the owner. If the customer doesn't like it, he can go somewhere else."

He's even got a big porcelain tile with that slogan on it hanging over the bar, right next to a picture of his five kids, that says under it: "Daddy, slow down!" He doesn't have a car and he doesn't even know how to drive, but he's always been jealous of my dad, because he's a truck driver and he can take the Bozo and me for rides.

That Saturday, January 7, all of Carabanchel was at Stumbles. People brought chairs in from other bars. It was incredible. And there I was, pretending that I liked soccer. (I've been pretending for as long as I can remember, and all so that my dad won't disinherit me.) It would really bug me if the Bozo were the one who got to keep my dad's truck. That's why I've spent my whole existence unable to confess that I have no idea what's going on when I watch a game.

I have to pretend like I understand if I want to be somebody in this life.

When they score I go into this crazy-fan mode. I yell more than anyone else, and that's how I save face, even though there are times when you can screw up and then your cover's blown. That's what happened that famous afternoon, when I went way over the top.

That mistake could have cost me my life. When Real Madrid scored the fourth goal, I got up on my chair, I took a deep breath, and with all my might, I yelled:

"Everybody, now: 'Three cheers for Messi!'"

I yelled with such force that my glasses got all fogged up and I couldn't see all the faces that had turned around to look at me. I did hear the "deafening silence." The deadly silence. I wiped off my glasses to see what was going on. They stopped looking at me and looked at my dad, like when the people in a bar in the West look up at a stranger who just came into the saloon. Those people wanted my dad to give me what I deserved, but my dad is against physical violence, and the only thing I could do was lower my head in shame. It was horrible—I felt like I do when I get chewed out, but at Stumbles they don't settle for the classic psychological humiliation. I looked around for my grandpa so he could defend me, but at that crucial moment in my life he was sleeping in the corner. So Ozzy broke the ice. He punched me, but not really hard, because my dad was there. It was a clean shot, and it gave me time to take off my glasses first. I felt like saying thanks to him. My dad said to Ozzy's dad, "Is your kid ever going to stop hitting my poor son?"

Manolito Four-Eyes

And Ozzy's dad said, "Manolo, you gotta admit that this time Manolito earned it. You can't let a child go out in public if he doesn't know that Messi's on Barcelona's team. For the love of God, it's common knowledge! It would be a tragedy if he scored. Plus there hasn't been any real harm; his glasses are intact and the physical damage isn't of any importance. For once my Ozzy has acted in an irreproachable fashion. Manolo, tell the kid either he gets up to speed or his days at Stumbles are over."

My dad was going to answer back, but then Real Madrid scored their fifth goal, and the customers forgot all about the psychological damage, which was what had hurt the most.

I wanted to forget about the whole episode in hopes that Ozzy would forget about it, too, even though I was sure that on Monday the entire school was going to find out about my screwup.

When we got home, my dad came in to say good

night, and he said, "Don't worry, Manolito. Tomorrow I'll teach you Real Madrid's lineup; that way nobody will be able to raise their voice or their fist at you again."

Everything went dark and a while went by. I thought I was the only one awake in the worldwide world, but then my grandpa said, "Manolito, warm up my feet."

We turned over on our sides, the same sides we always sleep on.

"Manolito, don't worry. During the next game, after we eat our *tortillas de patata*, you can come over to the corner with me and we can sleep through the whole game. When you do that, nobody even notices you."

"Grandpa, you don't care about anything in life."

"Just two things: you and the Bozo."

My grandpa, Supergrandpa, has always been on my team. I noticed he was falling asleep so I shook him a little so I could ask him a burning question that had been troubling me for some time.

"Grandpa, but you care about me more than the Bozo, right?"

"A little more, yeah, but don't go telling anyone."

A minute later I heard his first snore, and I put my hand in his mouth to take out his dentures. I said, "Grandpa, what would you do without me?"

And he answered with a snore that shook all of Carabanchel.

Misery Loves Company

This weekend, I'm not getting any allowance, and I won't be allowed to watch cartoons. So what? I'm the happiest guy alive right now in the worldwide world.

How is it possible—you and all of humanity might be wondering—that there's someone so crazy that he'd be happy with no money to buy candy and no TV?

It's true any normal person would feel pretty sorry for himself in my place. Even I would feel sorry for myself if it weren't for the fact that . . . I'm not the only one in the apartment who's grounded. For the first time in the history of my life, I'm sharing my punishment with my dear younger brother, the Bozo.

Usually they just ground me, and when they do, the one I hate the most is the Bozo—more than my mom, and that's saying a lot, because she's the one who grounds me. Don't ask me why I feel that way; it's one of those unsolved mysteries of science.

But this time is different. I will start from the beginning of time. . . .

So it turns out that the Bozo is a kid that, at four years of age, can't control his bodily functions the way my mother would like. I will say it in scientific terms so that you understand: the Bozo wets his bed. My mom has tried to remedy this with traditional methods; in other words, yelling down the hall, "Not again! We're going to go broke with all the detergent this kid is wasting! I'm going to make him sleep in the toilet!"

But she never follows through with her threats. The Bozo keeps sleeping in his gigantic crib, he keeps wetting his sheets, and my mom keeps yelling down the hall every morning at eight. This is the wonderful way the García Morenos greet every new day of the calendar year. By the way my mom screams, you'd think she was going to grab the Bozo by his feet and throw him down the stairwell. But she doesn't. After her screaming fit, she picks him up and, in the same hallway where she was just insulting him, smothers him with these suction-cup kisses (like an anteater), which the Bozo tolerates without saying a word because he's momma's little boy.

This scene had been performed for several centuries up until the other day when Our Nosy Neighbor Luisa came over and told my mom that, the day before, she'd called a radio program called *A Solution for Every Problem* and

asked the host, "Look, sir, I'm Bernabé's wife, aka Our Nosy Neighbor Luisa, and this is my problem: my neighbor, who is a good friend of mine, screams like she's possessed every morning because her son can't control his bodily functions. I'm desperate. What can I do?"

And the radio host man answered:

"Let's get right to the heart of the issue: this child is wetting his bed uncontrollably. This child has a psychic-psychological problem, and you have to take him to see a specialist right away. There's no time to lose."

When Our Nosy Neighbor Luisa got done telling us the unpleasant advice from the radio host man, my mom said with tears in her eyes, "I knew the poor little guy wasn't wetting his bed just for fun."

The next day we all went to see Miss Espe, the school psychologist. It was me, my mom, Luisa, my grandpa, and the Bozo. There were so many of us that poor Miss Espe had to stand. It was pretty fun. My grandpa sat in this chair with wheels that Miss Espe has, and at the end of the visit, he said to Miss Espe, "Do you mind giving me a little push up to the door? I've always wondered what it will feel like the day my legs give out and I have to be in a wheelchair."

It was one of those classic whoppers my grandpa tells. He always comes up with stuff like that whenever he likes a girl, and he likes Miss Espe.

Me and the Bozo lined up to help Miss Espe push the chair, and we ended up pushing my grandpa right into the door. He got a bump on his forehead, but he said it was worth it.

So, back to what I was saying. Miss Espe said she didn't know how to treat kids who wet their beds uncontrollably, so she gave us the address of a very distinguished hypnotist doctor.

The next afternoon, the same lot of us went to see the hypnotist doctor. We went in Luisa's car. She just got her driver's license and wanted to use us as guinea pigs. After being insulted by practically every driver on the road, and after performing an emergency parking job—in other words, ramming into the car in back and then into the car in front—we went up to the hypnotist doctor's office, which was in his house. It was the most luxurious house I'd ever seen in my whole life. The hypnotist doctor wouldn't let us all into his office. Me and my grandpa stayed out in the waiting room, but it was neat; we ate a whole tray full of candy that was on the table. My mom came out of the visit as white as a ghost and my grandpa said, "The doctor made a mistake and hypnotized your mom instead."

But it wasn't that—it was that the hypnotist was super expensive. The color in my mom's cheeks didn't come back till she was in Luisa's car riding with the window down and the wind hitting her face. It cost so much that we didn't stop at a café on the way home to get something to eat, which is what we always do when we go downtown.

Later, when night had fallen on the García Moreno residence, the moment of truth arrived: the moment when we were going to find out if the doctor's hypnotic words had left an impression in the Bozo's head.

It must have been around four in the morning when the Bozo started feeling that tingling sensation. When he got up and went down the hall toward the bathroom, what did my mom do? She followed him. Well, in my apartment if you want to follow someone, you have to do it with your eyes. It's too small for traditional following on foot. So she saw that the Bozo stopped right in front of the bathroom door, and he stood there for a minute, thinking in the dark like a monstrous child. My mom and the worldwide world were waiting for the Bozo to go over to the toilet. But he didn't. The Bozo turned right around and went back to his bed. What for? To wet his bed, which is where he likes to do it. That's my brother for you.

Conclusion: the Bozo got up following the orders of the mental alarm clock that had been planted in his brain by the doctor, but then he thought better of it, and the orders that had gone in one ear that afternoon went out the other ear at four in the morning. (Usually orders like

these take less time to travel this route in his head, but it was a nice gesture toward my mom, considering the expenses involved.) And the thing is, the Bozo isn't fond of change. He is happy with his pacifier, his crib, and his uncontrollable bodily functions.

The next day, my mom was in a rage when she got up. She blamed Luisa for all the money she'd thrown away on the hypnotist, and for the first time in her life, she punished the Bozo.

Seeing the Bozo punished made me want to laugh, jump, live life intensely—you know, normal stuff. Then the kid started crying because I was making fun of him. Can you believe it? Just because I was teasing him a little. And then they grounded me, too. Me, someone who has controlled his bodily functions since he was two months old, and I'm not exaggerating. Well, there's always an upside to everything, I'm happy that he's grounded, and he's happy that I'm grounded. This double punishment thing is bringing us closer. Whatever wise man said, "Misery loves company" was right on the money. He must've had a little brother.

5

Winners and Losers

One day, Miss Asunción said that we kids spend every afternoon thinking only about what's right in front of our noses—in other words, the TV.

"That's not true, Miss," said Arturo Román, who's always dying to talk. "I don't just think about the TV that's in front of my face; I also think about the TV that's in front of my friends' faces, and that maybe they're watching better programs, and I suffer because I don't have five TVs and five pairs of eyes."

For once, Arturo Román had hit the nail right on the head. There are afternoons when Big Ears López calls me and he's like, "Did you see *Knight Rider* on Channel Three?"

And I go, "No, I was watching *MacGyver* on Channel Five."

"*Knight Rider* is a whole lot cooler than *MacGyver*. MacGyver is a dork with a thug's haircut."

"That gorilla that drives the talking car is so much more of a thug. *Knight Rider* and its little music—duh-duh-na-na-duh-na-na—makes me wanna barf."

We hang up the phone without saying good-bye. We wait awhile, each one in the loneliness of our own home, going over and over in our minds the words that have been exchanged. One of us finally gives in and calls the other one. We do it so we can find out what's happening on the show we're not watching.

I gotta admit, there are times in life when our brains just can't work any harder.

Miss Asunción decided to intervene in order to avoid what she calls "the dumbing down of our minds." Our Teach told us that, from now on, kids in Carabanchel were going to have extracurricular activities that would make us forget about TV and that would turn us into creative kids, like the ones in the movies.

And here is where this story begins (and it doesn't end too well, I'm warning you). I'll start the story from the beginning of time. . . .

A boy and girl came to our school and hung up a poster that said:

*SIGN UP FOR A CREATIVITY
WORKSHOP WITH YOUR FRIENDS, FAME
AND CRONOPIOS! THIS SUNDAY IS
THE FIRST RECYCLED ART CONTEST IN
PEDRO SALINAS PARK.
HEY, DUDE, DON'T MISS IT!*

Big Ears asked, "Where's that park at?"

Miss Asunsión told us it was the place we called Hangman's Park and that we oughta call things by their proper names.

We all watched how Fame (the girl) and Cronopios (the boy) hung up the poster. They weren't brother and sister, but they were dressed the same, in these baggy jean overalls, and they both had hair in their armpits (their underarms, so we're clear). That caught our attention, the girl having hair there and all. My mom makes sure every single hair is gone. Our Nosy Neighbor Luisa comes up every month with her Depilady and psuh! Psuh! Goodbye, hair! All the kids' moms in my class do the same thing. It must be a tradition in Carabanchel.

The day of the Recycled Art Contest finally arrived. The slogan was "Turn your trash into art." The organizers gave us half an hour to go through all the trash bins to get stuff to make an unforgettable work of art. My mom went to the drugstore and got me and the Bozo some masks and surgical gloves. It was our uniform as trash handlers. The Bozo was in the Illiterate category. (That's a joke. Man, I have to explain everything!) Ozzy was in that category, too. (No, that's not true, either, but it should have been like that.)

Fame and Cronopios said, "Go," and we all took off, pushing and shoving, which is our style. Our parents stayed in the park, and while we were out rummaging through trash bins, Fame and Cronopios organized games so they were entertained.

When we got back, they were doing the chair one: where the music plays and you gotta go around and around the chairs, and then the music stops and you sit down in the first chair you can grab, and the person still standing is out and gets super peeved.

Anyway, Luisa and my mom were about to get physical over a chair. My dad and her husband, Bernabé, had to pull them apart. It was getting really ugly; I'm not kidding.

The Bozo and I came back loaded down with all our trash: some egg shells (there was an obese fly drowning in one of them), chicken bones, toilet paper rolls, and some empty wine boxes that the owner of Stumbles gave us. Our trash bag was overflowing. The Bozo and I made a ship, and we gave it a really poetic title: *Something Is Rotten in the State of Carabanchel.*

I had to take the Bozo's pacifier away from him because he was about to dip it in the cream still left on the Twinkie wrapper we used for the sails. There's just no hope for that kid, I swear.

We were sure we were going to win. We were so sure

because Ozzy, who was acting even tougher than usual, had gotten a trash can from his mom and had titled it *Typical Trash Can.* The nerve of some people.

Big Ears' project was gross. He had brought some moldy cheese and brown lettuce that was in the One-and-Only Susana's entryway and named it *Chef's Salad.*

Susana had asked for some chicken legs at the supermarket, and she'd put them in a plastic jar, like they were flowers. Her work was called *Rest in Peace.* The audience made a gagging sign.

Cronopios and Fame went around looking at all our creations. They told me and the Bozo that ours was very interesting and that we had made a big creative effort. My mom yelled from her seat, "That's 'cause these kids have a limitless imagination."

Victory was ours. All ours. That's why, when Cronopios and Fame, after talking amongst themselves, announced with two little grins that they had decided that there weren't going to be any winners or losers, that "we all used our talent to the max," and that we all deserved the sought-after win, me and the Bozo, along with Our Nosy Neighbor Luisa, went over to the organizers to protest. In Carabanchel, we just don't get this thing about everybody winning.

Ozzy wanted the winner to be announced, too. We all demanded that there be a first place, and a second, and a third. With the medal, and the podium, and the national anthem—the whole nine yards. Like in the Olympics.

Anybody who wants a consolation prize can go somewhere else. Those kinds of prizes just aren't our style, buddy.

Ozzy the Bully, the biggest bully ever, had a fit and yanked off one of our Twinkie sails. Believe it or not, I have my limits, so I kicked his can. The can knocked Big Ears' chef's salad on the ground. We started throwing our works of art in each other's faces. The Bozo armed himself with a pan that Arturo Román had brought for his project: *The Chickens Have Come Home to Roast*. The Bozo was swinging the pan around and ended up whacking me in the face, right smack on the forehead. The pan missed my glasses by about a half an inch. As you can see, I'm always one to look on the bright side of things in life.

Fame and Cronopios joined the party (by this time the

little grins were gone from their faces) and asked Miss Asunción to get us under control.

"Me?" said Our Teach, without budging. "I don't work on Saturdays. I close the police station and leave my stick and whistle at home."

"We're never coming back to this park ever again. What a bunch of delinquents!" said Fame, pulling out a chicken leg that had come flying through the air during the fight and landed in her hair.

They got in their "Fame and Cronopios: Creativity Workshop" truck and zoomed away, peeling out like they do in the movies.

Little by little, the parents were able to separate us from our rivals, but not before Big Ears, who was giggling uncontrollably from his great idea, put pieces of cheese on Susana's legs (I mean her chicken's legs) and used them as a catapult.

None of the parents understood why Fame and Cronopios had gotten so mad. They're used to all our cultural events failing on the organization side.

That afternoon my mom put on the video of *E.T.* for us for the fifteenth time while my parents took a nap. The Bozo and I cried because that Martian reminds us of our grandpa when he takes out his dentures after he's had three glasses of wine and points to our block and says, "Home," thinking he'll never be able to make it back up to the sofa bed.

Down the street, in Hangman's Park, my grandpa was

soaking up some rays, surrounded by trash—or thousands of works of art. Bernabé said that it looked like the city dump or the Reina Sofía art museum, depending on how you looked at it.

6

Piggies

Up until a year and a half ago, I thought Our Nosy Neighbor Luisa possessed one of the largest fortunes in the country. You would've thought so, too, if you'd seen her five-speed blender, her super-duper mixer, and her super-sonic vacuum. But my mom told me the Truth about Life:

"The problem with Luisa is that she exaggerates a lot."

And my grandpa told me more of the Truth about Life:

"In any case, Manolito, keep in mind that having more money than we do is not hard. In fact, it's a piece of cake."

The Truth about Life is horrible. It's better not to know it.

So the day Luisa came up to our apartment to tell us that Bernabé had gotten a raise and that she wanted us to give a small but meaningful party in his honor—and my mom screamed with uncontrollable delight—I didn't know whether Luisa was exaggerating or my mom was a really fake person. Once again, I was wrong. My mom told me it was true, that up until then Bernabé had been the representative for whole olives, and that from now on, he would also be the rep for olives on a stick, and for eggplant in vinegar, and pitted olives, and olives stuffed with anchovies. That last type of olive is cultivated only in Spain. Don't ask me how it's possible for farmers to grow olives with anchovies in them. Nobody knows how the anchovies get in there. They've even held conferences and

41

invited American scientists who study this type of olive, and they haven't found the answer. The farmers aren't saying a word. It's as big a mystery as the formula for Coca-Cola.

The truth is, it was a big deal that Bernabé was now the rep for stuffed olives. First of all, because from that moment on we wouldn't have to put up with the Bozo choking every five minutes on the pit; and second, because Bernabé was going to earn more money, and since he's my godfather and on top of that he doesn't have any kids, he told me that he's keeping me in mind for his will, even if my mom and Luisa say that you don't talk about w-i-l-l-s when the k-i-d-s are around. (The k-i-d-s are me and the Bozo.)

Having Bernabé as my godfather is a whole lotta cool. When we get together at Christmas or for Carabanchel parties at Stumbles, he ends up dancing the conga, and he lets me and the Bozo hold his toupee because his head sweats a lot. Luisa doesn't like the fact that Bernabé goes around letting people hold his toupee, because he got it in a Frank Sinatra store on Grand Street and it cost a lot of money. So, check it out, my godfather wears the same toupee as Frank Sinatra. Now that I think about it, he's not just a whole lotta cool, he's a super whole lotta cool.

Me and the Bozo went with Luisa and my mom to the store to buy the delicacies for this meaningful party. We put the Bozo in the shopping cart so that he wouldn't get lost, but since he started jumping on the eggs, we had to put him on the ground. Consequence: he got lost in five minutes. My mom asked the lady in charge of lost children if she could use the microphone to call him over the loud-speaker.

"Son, come back. I have a Kit Kat for you."

It's mathematical: five seconds later, the Bozo comes out from behind the floor display. My mom chews him out real bad, then the Bozo cries, and my mom gives him the Kit Kat and then some suction-cup kisses. We have this act down pat—the Bozo getting lost and then being rescued. We rehearse it about once a week, and I must say, it's pretty good.

We went back to Luisa's with all the delicacies, and Luisa fixed up the dining room (which is reserved for important events) and put some big candlesticks on the table, which didn't leave any room for the delicacies. My grandpa said that, a year ago, he dreamed that he saw Luisa on the stairs in her nightgown and she was carrying one of those candlesticks, and he still gets the chills when he thinks about it.

Luisa said Bernabé didn't know we were all invited to this small but meaningful party, and that my godfather is a very simple man and he doesn't want to go around say-ing he got promoted.

"He doesn't have to—you do it for him."

I said that, and I didn't mean anything by it; I swear with my hand on the Bible. I said it because I felt it. My mom and dad shoved their elbows in my mouth. One day they're going to have to buy me some false teeth, and they'll be really sorry because a kid with false teeth is a pretty sad thing.

At 8:05 p.m., we heard the keys. Bernabé walked in. We were all quiet. The Bozo whispered to me, "Baby wants the pit."

Would you believe he was actually entertaining himself by opening up olives and looking for the pits? He doesn't want to let go of the tradition of choking. It's part of his identity.

Bernabé yelled from the door, "Piggy, are you there?"

We almost died laughing. We never could have imagined that Our Nosy Neighbor Luisa was . . . Piggy.

Luisa glared at us. "Yes, I'm here!" she yelled.

I expected her to add "Kermit." But what my godfather did next proved that "Piggy" was the most appropriate name for him, too. What happened next will go down in Carabanchel history, and I was a firsthand witness: Bernabé farted all the way down the hall. They were these thunderous farts, farts that didn't seem possible coming out of someone as small as Bernabé, out of a person with a toupee. These farts were superhuman. For a minute I felt a chill all over my body. What if Bernabé had turned into a monster? I think we all felt the same way, starting with Luisa, who was as red as a tomato, followed by my parents and my grandpa, who were all looking in different directions. My dad was staring at an electrical outlet, my mom was staring at her fork, and my grandpa was staring at the ground and biting his lower lip with all his might. The only one who continued in his normal state (to call his state "normal" is a bit of an exaggeration) was the Bozo, who kept looking for the pits in the olives.

Bernabé hadn't turned into a monster. But when he got to the dining room and saw us all there in silence, he turned totally red. He looked like the Mickey Mouse that the Bozo has on his nightstand, whose face lights up so that the Bozo's not scared at night.

Bernabé just stood there for about thirty seconds and then said, "Man, don't you hate it when your lunch doesn't agree with you?"

Then a really strange thing happened: everybody pretended like the terrifying farts never happened. We had dinner, and they gave me and the Bozo a tiny bit of champagne when they toasted to Bernabé's promotion. Bernabé let us wear his toupee, and he walked us to the door, dancing the conga. Before we went upstairs, my godfather gave me a kiss and reminded me about his will, and Luisa and my mom yelled at him, like always.

Nobody's ever made a joke in front of Bernabé about that day when his lunch didn't agree with him. But that night when my mom and I went to our gigantic baby's crib to tell him a story like we do every night, and my mom said, "Which one do you want tonight?" the Bozo, who's a jokester even if he doesn't realize it, said, "The little piggies."

"This little piggy went to market; this little piggy stayed home; this little piggy had roast beef; this little piggy . . ."

But she couldn't finish because she was laughing so hard, so my dad came in and he tried, and the same thing happened, and then my grandpa, whose dentures came out of place because he was dying laughing. The Bozo was clapping and jumping up and down watching the three of them lying on the bed, splitting their sides with laughter.

I was watching them, too, and I didn't want that moment ever to end. I wanted it to last forever.

7

A Spoonful of Sugar

I don't know what your parents do on a typical Friday night, but mine go down to Our Nosy Neighbor Luisa's to see R-rated movies.

Usually they put the Bozo in bed with me so I can take care of him in case he chokes. We have an awesome time. If my grandpa graces us with one of his super snores (which, on a good night, can wake up our upstairs neighbor), we get the giggles; if we have a farting contest, we get the giggles; and if we stare at our toes, we get the giggles. Those are our three main varieties of entertainment on Friday nights. That's it. Every once in a while the Bozo chokes, I give him a whack on the back, and then he coughs with all his might, and we get the giggles again.

This is how we spend our time.

But last night was different, because the Bozo was sick (once again, his classic mega-production of boogers); and when he's sick, my parents leave him *incomunicado* in his crib because two kids with that disgusting virus would be like a horror movie.

I had to take care of him and give him a spoonful of medicine at the exact time that my mom had set the alarm to go off. The Bozo, even though he's four, still sleeps in a crib. He's so big his feet hang out through the bars. He looks like this humongous baby. Sometimes I have night-mares about him.

It sucks taking care of the Bozo. Well, "sucks" is the scientific expression. The more popular expression is, "It is unpleasant taking care of the Bozo." And my mom makes me do it because she doesn't trust my grandpa, because my grandpa sleeps in chunks during the night, and if the chunk when he's sleeping coincides with the one where he has to give the Bozo his cough syrup, we're in trouble. My grandpa says he has insomnia, and my mom tells Luisa that he has it because he sleeps all day long. First, he takes a nap in Hangman's Park. Ever since Ozzy's grandpa and mine bought their sweatsuits, they put in their false teeth, put on their sweatsuits, their berets, and their scarves, and go down to take their morning nap—just killing time till we get out of school for lunch. Then, after lunch, he sleeps through two soap operas with the Bozo, and then he also sleeps in the evening through whatever program is on TV.

On top of having slept all day, he gets up to go to the bathroom all night long because he's got prostate problems. Result: he can't concentrate and he sleeps in chunks.

My parents went to the store in the afternoon to buy toilet paper for the whole weekend, and my mom said, "Remember, Manolito, six cc's at six."

We always talk like that in my family. We're like a bunch of scientists, just a little scruffier.

So anyway, six o'clock rolls around. I go and grab the little syrup cup, and I pour six cc's. So far, so good. I go to the living room. My grandpa's there sleeping through a documentary on the reproduction of cockroaches, and the Bozo's pretending like he understands it. He's such a phony. When he saw me with the little cup, the Bozo started wailing. He's impossible when it comes to cough syrup. I left to go back to the kitchen again, the whole time doing a balancing act so I wouldn't spill the healing liquid, and then I appeared again in the living room without the little cup. I said to the Bozo, "Shut up, party pooper. You're going to wake up grandpa, and he's sleeping through this terrific documentary."

That said, I yanked his pacifier out of his mouth. I didn't do it to be mean; I did it because when you take away his pacifier, he follows you around the whole apartment. He followed me to the kitchen. I sat him down in his highchair and when he saw the little cup, that humongous four-year-old baby started howling again, waving his arms and kicking left and also right. He slapped the little

cup and it went flying out of my hands, and he knocked over the cough syrup bottle that was on the table. Bye-bye, syrup.

We just sat there looking at the mess for two and a half minutes (you could cut the tension with a knife), till I said, "Now what do we do, Bozo?"

I knew my mom was going to see the empty bottle and end up blaming me. She always believes the Bozo. He's the apple of her eye, and I'm the orange.

I cleaned up all the sticky mess left by the syrup, which wasn't easy. Then I said to the Bozo, "And now what do we fill the bottle with, Genius?"

These are things I say affectionately, believe me. If he weren't my brother, I wouldn't treat him in such a loving way. But let's get back to that desperate moment and that empty bottle. My head went to work. Since the syrup was pink, I mixed strawberry jam, milk, and sugar. (The sugar I added just to make it more interesting.) I shook the bottle, and the little guy drank his six cc's without talking back. After licking his upper lip and his bottom lip, he said, "Baby wants more."

He always talks like that, in the third person. He's a very strange child.

"Well, Baby's gonna have to deal with it," I said, "because Mom said only six cc's."

After I said that, I lifted the cup to my lips and gulped down six cc's myself. I wasn't sick but "an ounce of prevention is worth a pound of cure," as some famous American guy once said.

Later that night, as I already said, I went to take care of the Bozo in his crib, while my parents were watching R-rated movies at Luisa's apartment and my grandpa was sleeping in one of his famous chunks. You can't imagine how much the little guy loved his new syrup. He was just staring at the clock, without blinking, waiting for the alarm to go off so he could have another cupful.

One cupful, then another, then another . . . and eventually we finished off the whole bottle. Then I filled it up again with my special invention so there would be no trace of our actions. In all, we drank at least three bottles each.

The Bozo's throat got better. The typical "gazebo" effect worked. It's an effect that scientists from all over the world have studied, that basically means any medicine can cure you even if it's fake, if you have faith. (Paquito Medina says this is really called the "placebo" effect, but whatever.) The Bozo has a lot of faith. His throat doesn't hurt him anymore today, the boogers are gone, but now the sickness has gone to his stomach. In other words, he has a tummy ache. My mom said, "I never get a break with this kid; if it's not one thing it's another."

Today my parents went to the movies. My grandpa is sleeping through a prostate operation that Luisa taped for him on the TV, and I can't stop thinking about the new syrup Dr. Morales gave the Bozo. It's the color of poop— so we understand each other. I don't think I can pull another *switch-a-rooney*, but the Bozo looked at me with that look of his and said, "Baby wants syrup, but he wants the one Manolito makes."

And I can't resist. There are times when I think I'm actually kind of fond of the Bozo. I'm a sentimental kid; what can I say?

8

A Clear Conscience

By now, on every street corner in Carabanchel they're talking about the crime I committed. A small piece of advice: if you want to keep a secret, go live in another neighborhood; in this one it's impossible.

The funniest thing about it is I swear that I didn't commit any crime, and to this day, no one believes me. I will begin my terrifying story from the beginning of time. . . .

After lunch me and Big Ears were out staining our T-shirts (we were eating ice cream) when from far away we saw Ozzy sitting on the bench in Hangman's Park.

"Aw, man, there's Ozzy, what a bore," said Big Ears.

"Yeah, a bore galore," I said. I'm a stickler for precision

when it comes to language.

Having said that, we started walking over toward Ozzy. Yeah, it's true. Nobody understands us. Anyone else would have turned right around and gone the other way. Anyone else would have had more self-respect.

"Well looky here, it's Four-Eyes and Big Ears. Naughty, naughty, your mommies are gonna have to wash your shirts."

Ozzy's the same age as us, but he likes to bully us as if he were older and he hangs out with guys that go to the Tech School. Lately, he's been wearing two earrings in the same ear and his hat on backward. He doesn't hang out with us because he doesn't consider us cool enough. So when he told us to sit down next to him, we were crazy excited. I told you: we have no self-respect.

Ozzy told us he was waiting for some guys from the Tech School to have a little friendly soccer match.

"You guys can stay and watch."

We were about to say thanks, when he did something that left our jaws hanging pretty open: he pulled out a pack of cigarettes from his back pocket and put one in his mouth.

"I'd ask if you guys wanted one, but kids don't smoke."

When Ozzy bullies me and Big Ears like that, we get this classic idiot smile on our faces. I know: anyone else would have walked away, but we're heroes of the resistance.

"Look how I light the match."

Ozzy took the match, flicked it with his nail, and it

lighted. Me and Big Ears both said, "Cool!" at the same time.

Then he put the burning side of the cigarette in his mouth and didn't make a face or anything. He even blew out smoke as if it were nothing.

"Cool!" (That was us again.)

He started blowing rings with the smoke. He showed us how you can blow it out of your nose and talk with the cigarette on one side of your mouth. And after every demonstration, Big Ears and I said, "Cool!"

Then the Tech guys showed up, all wearing their hats backward, and Ozzy got up and ran over to them. Big Ears turned his hat around, and I was like, "You're such a brown-noser."

At that moment I considered myself a kid with values, a kid with his hat on right, with the bill forward, a kid who wasn't easily bribed.

Ozzy came back over to where we were.

"We're gonna warm up for a while. Either one of you want to volunteer to hold my cigarette?"

I'm embarrassed to say it, but you can't change history: Big Ears and I raised our hands really high, like we knew the answer to one of Miss Asunción's questions at school. Just thinking about it makes me want to barf.

"We can take turns." That great idea came from Big Ears.

"Yeah, yeah, we can take turns!" The memory of that sentence torments me to this day.

"Well, all right. And no fighting, eh?" Every once in a while, Ozzy likes to pretend he's our dad.

If Big Ears and I had been two dogs, we would've wagged our tails.

"And who's gonna go first?" asked Big Ears.

"So there are no problems, we're going to do it in strict alphabetical order," said Ozzy. "First López and then García."

"But *L* comes after *G*!" I have my limits, believe it or not.

"Well, whatever. First López. See? That's what you get for trying to be a wise guy, Manolito," said the big boss.

He gave Big Ears the cigarette and went to kick the ball around. The Tech kids weren't passing it to him, so Ozzy came over once in a while to take a puff.

"Now it's Four-Eyes' turn."

Finally, it was my turn! Not to brag or anything, but I was holding that cigarette like I'd been smoking my whole life, like a master. I'm just very observant; what can I say?

I was no longer that kid with values I'd been a moment ago, and I put my hat on backward. I thought that if, at that moment, a talent scout had walked by Hangman's Park, he would've hired me on the spot.

"Hey, kid, you got any acting experience?" the scout would say to me.

"What's experience when you've got natural talent?" I'd answer with the cigarette in my hand.

But big movie producers don't usually go by my park.

It's not on their way. Someone whose way it *is* on is my mom, who comes down with the Bozo every afternoon to give him his yogurt. The Bozo, instead of eating his yogurt with sugar, likes to have it with dirt. His behavior is a little extravagant. So I wasn't surprised when I saw them. What surprised me was that my mom came running over to where I was. Her look was horrible, one of those looks that would make any son shudder. You could see she wasn't running over to tell me how much she loved me. I thought, "What could I have done that's so bad in the last twenty-four hours?" That's the worst thing that can happen to you in this life, knowing you're going to get in trouble and not even knowing why.

My mom stopped in front of me, breathing hard like those women in the movies who get mad with all their heart.

"What are you doing with that cigarette in your hand?"

Oh, so *that* was it. Luckily, my mom was wrong for once and she had taken me for something I'm not: a chain-smoker.

"I was just holding it for Ozzy."

But my mom's expression didn't change. She was kind of growling, showing her teeth and all, like Our Nosy Neighbor Luisa's dog when she wants to fight. I was going to have to explain it to her more clearly.

"First Big Ears held it, and now it's my turn." I didn't know there was anything wrong with holding a cigarette for a friend.

My mom called Ozzy over.

"Ozzy, is this your cigarette?"

Ozzy came over, shook his head, and ran back over with his buddies.

"Don't look at me," said Big Ears, looking up at my mom. "I don't know anything about that cigarette."

"Dirty traitor," I thought to myself, glaring at Big Ears.

My mom said, "Put your hat on right. You look like a hooligan."

I put my hat on with the bill toward the front, hoping she would just leave it at that. But it was only the beginning. She started in on one of her famous lectures.

Afterward, it was impossible to convince her that I hadn't been smoking. She gets an idea in her head, and nobody can change her mind.

My dad gave me a man-to-man talk, and he said the day I wanted to smoke that I should do it in my own apartment that I bought with my own money. Oh, brother.

Our Nosy Neighbor Luisa brought up a medical pamphlet on how to quit smoking.

The Bozo, who always wants to imitate me, pretended like he was smoking his pacifier.

And my grandpa, after we got into bed, said, "You take after your old grandpa, you know? Sense of humor, irony . . . You know that when your mom catches me smoking in the bar, I tell her I was just holding the cigarette for someone else?"

"Grandpa, I'm innocent."

"Sure you are, buddy. How could a ten-year-old not be innocent. . . ?"

I knew then that nobody would ever believe me, and like a criminal who serves an unjust and cruel sentence, I fell asleep. But right before I did, I thought about what my grandpa has told me many times: "The most important thing in life is having a clear conscience."

I was the only one who had a clear conscience and the only one who had gotten chewed out, so I don't understand what the point is of having a clear conscience if nobody else believes it. I don't think Big Ears or Ozzy care much about this conscience thing. They don't have consciences.

I started imagining revenge. Getting back at Big Ears was pretty easy. If I don't talk to him the whole morning or if I don't give him half of my sandwich (he always forgets his), he gets all dramatic. But I wouldn't be able to get back at Ozzy until many years later when I became the owner of a big company, and he came to ask me for a job. What if I never became the owner of a big company, and he never came to ask me for a job? Then I'd just have to suck it up.

That night I dreamed I was a gangster. I was wearing a dark suit with white stripes, and a hat, and black-and-white shoes. Big Ears was the bartender, and I snapped my fingers so he'd bring me another Coke. The One-and-Only Susana was next to me in a long dress, and she said,

"I always liked you best, Manolito. Your intelligence out-shines anyone else's in the gang. That's why you're the boss, *il capo*."

I smiled, knowing that she was right, and I took a puff on this enormous candy cigar I was holding.

"Watch and learn," I said to Susana, and I blew huge pink smoke rings that turned into hearts.

"Cool!" said Susana with great admiration.

Then I tapped the cigar so that the pink ash would fall. But it didn't fall on the floor. It fell on Ozzy's head, who, by the way in case I failed to mention it, was shining my shoes.

It was the best dream of my life. Dreams are what make life worth living.

Baby's Not Bald

My friends'll never admit it, but I know they're jealous of me. They're jealous of the huge truck I will have one day. They're jealous that when my dad comes home on Friday nights after his long trips, as soon as he pulls onto our street, he honks twice so we know that he's here. But we're not the only ones; everybody else knows, too.

The coolest thing is that there's a sacred rule that my mom has to let us go down to greet my dad no matter what time it is. It can catch you in the bathroom, having dinner, or in the bathtub, it doesn't matter; you gotta run downstairs as fast as you can, get there in time to open the truck door for him, and wrap yourself mercilessly around his neck. My dad goes up three flights of stairs with us hanging off him and says, "You guys are going to kill me. What does your mom give you to eat? You're getting fatter by the day."

The other day my dad's horn made the whole neighborhood shake at one o'clock in the morning. I woke up and jumped out of bed and put on my flip-flops. My mom didn't want to let me go down because she said at that time of night, it wasn't right for a kid to go walking around outside. I went over by the door, almost crying, and I would've gotten on my knees if necessary. "If he's honked, it means he wants us to come down!"

My grandpa yelled from bed, in that voice he has when he's not wearing his teeth, "Let the little guy go down and see his dad. You always gotta say no to everything!"

After hearing my grandpa yell, the Bozo started crying like a madman from his humongous crib. Since my mom wouldn't get him out, he took a nosedive onto the floor. While he was feeling the bump on his forehead, he pointed at me: "Baby wants go with Manolito!"

And out of fear of an uncontrollable nocturnal tantrum (known to be heard all the way in France), my mom put on our jackets over our pajamas and let us run downstairs. Our Nosy Neighbor Luisa, who's always on the lookout in case the enemy is lurking, came out when we got to her landing on the second floor. "Why in the world is your mom letting you out at this hour?"

"Because their dad's a troublemaker, and he honks the horn for them," said my mom, sticking her head out.

"Well, there are kids who have been kidnapped at their very own front door."

We heard the neighbor on the fourth floor yell down: "You think a kidnapper's gonna put up with these two? Could you make any more noise going down the stairs?"

"Go back to bed, you grump!" said Luisa.

"Lady, how can I get any sleep when your door is open to business all hours of the night?"

We went out on the street so I couldn't hear any more, but I think Luisa said he was confused and that his mom was the one with the nighttime business.

My dad was already parking the truck, and he shined his lights on us. My dad's truck can light up the entire street; that's been proven and signed by a notary. He opened the door and same as always, we threw ourselves at him like ticks, and we went up the stairs like that, each of us hanging off an arm.

My dad smelled like "Manolito" (which is also the name of his truck) and sweat. It's too bad he takes a shower when he gets home because I love that "welcome home" smell.

My mom tried to peel us off my dad. She said it was really late and why were we up? But we knew perfectly well that what she wanted was to be alone with him. She wanted him all for herself. But it was impossible. We caught him first. We weren't about to give up our prey: the big white elephant. So she had no choice but to let us stay while he had dinner. It was one thirty when my mom started making him dinner. With the sizzling of the eggs in the frying pan, my grandpa woke up. He always hears the sizzling and goes to the kitchen and plops down in a chair, and whatever is put in front of him, he dips his bread in and eats it. My mom said, "Dad, you already ate fried eggs two hours ago."

"What do you expect, for me to stay in bed while you guys are here eating behind my back?" My grandpa can get really dramatic when there are fried eggs involved.

"The only thing Manolo is going to eat is—"

"Baby wants like grapa," (grapa is my grandpa), the Bozo said, interrupting my mom and setting his pacifier on the table to get ready to gulp down whatever it was.

"Why don't you make eggs for everyone? I'm sick of eating alone all week." That's my dad, the one with the great ideas.

"At two in the morning?"

"That can easily be fixed. We won't have breakfast till noon tomorrow, and amen," said my grandpa.

A second later, Luisa rang the bell asking what all the racket was about. She wanted to know if something had happened. Five minutes later, there she was in her night-gown, dipping bread in everybody else's eggs. Bernabé came up to get her, and she shut him up by stuffing a piece of bread in his mouth. Between all of us, we finished a whole loaf, not counting the Bozo, of course. He doesn't use bread to dip; he uses his pacifier. He just wants to be different.

"Now that's what I call a fried egg, Catalina!" said my grandpa before going back to bed. He kept talking as he was going down the hall: "What a great idea eating eggs during the night. This is an experience I'm going to have to do again."

When we finished having dinner, my dad inspected us. He does that every Friday. The Bozo and I stand up real straight with our backs to the kitchen door, and he makes a mark with a pencil to see if we've grown while he was gone. We have to watch out because the minute we look away, the Bozo stands on his tiptoes. Lately, I've been a little worried because the distance between the Bozo's mark and mine is getting shorter and shorter. The truth is

I would not find it very amusing having a little brother taller than me. What a disgrace. I couldn't go out in public anymore.

Every once in a while, like that night, Dad says the magic words, "Catalina, these sheep need a shearin'."

As soon as our hair starts covering our ears, he takes us to his barber, Mr. Esteban. My dad says that Mr. Esteban is a master with scissors. Mr. Esteban has Parkinson's disease, which makes his hands shake, but he's never cut off any ears. If it's a baby with three little hairs on its head, or an old man with three little hairs on his head, when he gets close with his scissors, the baby cries, terrified, and the old man closes his eyes and says what he thinks are his last words. The rest of the people in the barber shop hold their breath and swallow hard. And what happens? Nothing happens. My grandpa says it's a haircut with excitement and suspense included in the price.

The next morning my parents went down to Stumbles to have their Saturday morning coffee. My dad said, "You guys come down in half an hour, and we'll go to Mr. Esteban's."

That was when I had the idea of the century: I would save my parents money by giving the Bozo a haircut myself. I mean, after all, it's not really worth it for so little hair. . . . It was going to be a big surprise. Everyone would say, "Wow, look how nice Mr. Esteban cut the little guy's hair!"

"It wasn't Mr. Esteban," my mom would say, "it was my Manolito."

I took the Bozo into the bathroom with me and sat him down on a stool. I consulted him first because I don't like to force anyone. "Does the baby wanna be handsome?"

"Baby handsome."

That meant he gave his consent. Only us experts understand his language.

Then the operation began. I wanted it to be perfect. I got a towel and put it on him like a cape. Then I gave him one of my mom's magazines to read, and he opened it to an article on Melanie Griffith and Antonio Banderas. He must've liked it because he didn't turn the page the whole time. Every once in a while, he'd point at Melanie and say, "Luisa."

He's very optimistic.

The moment of truth had arrived. I picked up the scissors and began my work of art. First I took off some of the curls in the back. I wanted to leave him a little rattail there like the one Ozzy had last year. But instead of being down at the bottom, the rattail was up really high. I stepped back to look at it. Well, it was fine. I got to work on the front. I took off a chunk of bangs on one side, then another chunk on the other. I'm not sure why, but it wasn't coming out even, so I kept cutting first on one side then on the other, back and forth like that for a while. Until I couldn't keep going because he didn't have any hair left. I started cutting the middle until I realized he was bald there, too. The only thing left on his head was that little curl in the back. All of a sudden the curl on that pink head looked like a little pig's tail. I can't really say he looked handsome. He looked . . . original.

"You like it? Doesn't the baby look original?"

The Bozo peered up from Melanie for a moment and stared at himself in the mirror: "Baby's bald."

"No he's not, see . . ." I gave him a little mirror so he could see the back, like they do at the hair salon, and I showed him his pigtail. He examined it carefully for a long while. Finally, he gave his approval: "Baby handsome."

He loved it. It was a good thing. He's a very demanding kid. But I wasn't so sure about it myself. I was scared that other people weren't going to value the originality of the haircut. Those other people I was scared of were waiting for us at the front door. They were . . . my parents.

My mom stared with her mouth wide open. The Bozo turned all the way around and, grabbing his pigtail, said, "Baby's not bald, Baby handsome."

"And original," I said with one of those smiles that nobody appreciates.

The consequences of my haircut were terrible: they grounded me all Saturday afternoon with no TV. But that wasn't the worst of it. I would have been able to accept that. The worst was that my mom cut off the Bozo's little pig's tail and he wouldn't stop crying. He wouldn't stop crying until he went to bed. And I'm not exaggerating.

10

Spain's Girlfriend

I'm a pretty optimistic guy, despite all the dirty tricks fate has played on me. For instance, the very first one, right off the bat: Why did I have to be born on August 10, a birthday I wouldn't wish on my worst enemy? If you're born on August 10, all your friends are on vacation. Who's gonna go to your birthday party? Our Nosy Neighbor Luisa and Bernabé, the Bozo, my grandpa, and my parents—that's who. Ah, and as a special guest, Big Ears, who I can't even get rid of to go to the bathroom (we usually go together). I already told you the very first dirty trick; now I'm going to tell you the latest one: Miss Asunción says that I'm not making adequate progress in math, and my mom likes to repeat that in front of other people to see if I get mad and, out of spite, turn into that perfect kid I've never been. It bothers me, but I don't let her break me.

So, as I said, I'm a born optimist. Nevertheless, there are things that totally get to me, like when Ozzy wins all the bottle caps that my grandpa just bought me the day before. He cleans me out in a second and then says, "You stink, Manolito."

Then he goes on to the next guy, who's usually Big Ears.

The other day, Ozzy won nine bottle caps off me in record time. And what did I do? I went over to the corner of the playground and thought about how I was going to turn into Zorro and take on that idiot in a sword fight. I'd pick him up by his coat with my sword and dangle him from Hangman's Tree till his mom found him. Actually, first my grandpa would see him, because he goes down to the park for a nap every morning. But my grandpa wouldn't help him down, because my grandpa holds even more of a grudge against Ozzy than I do, and that's saying a lot.

The Zorro thing suddenly seemed silly. I could never get even with anybody, so I resigned myself to hating Ozzy in silence and feeling sorry for myself for having the worst luck in the worldwide world.

I was in the middle of hating Ozzy when the One-and-Only Susana came over, handed me a piece of paper, smiled at me mysteriously, and walked away. At that low point in my life, I expected a message like: "You couldn't be more of a loser even if you tried."

But this is what I found:

> Four-eyes. You have been chosen out of many to celebrate my birthday with me next Monday. Don't rack your brain trying to come up with a gift. I was thinking it would be easier if you just gave me money. Do not talk to anyone about this!
>
> Susana

I was extremely moved. I just sat there with my mouth wide open. I think I even swallowed one of those huge flies that are always swarming around my school in the spring. They're part of the wildlife in my neighborhood, and we're lucky that they're not an endangered species. We can kill as many as we want; they reproduce like flies.

Well, you're probably thinking that I had this dumb look on my face. Frankly, you can think whatever you want. Ozzy and Big Ears came over to where I was.

"What did Susana want?" said Ozzy.

I closed my mouth and swallowed hard.

"Nothing. She wanted to know why I was over here in the corner all sad."

"What? Susana asked you why you were all sad? Ha! Susana doesn't care if you're sad. Susana didn't say that. What do you think, Big Ears?"

"I, uh . . ." Big Ears looked at me and then he looked at Ozzy. "No, I don't think that's what Susana said."

Ozzy pointed his finger at me and said in a pretty threatening voice, "See? Even your friend here doesn't think so. And he knows you better than anyone. . . . Be careful, Manolito. Susana's my girlfriend."

And he left, leaving Big Ears and me face-to-face.

"You're a dirty traitor," I said to Big Ears.

"What would you have done in my place?"

"I would've defended you."

That's a rotten lie. I'm a dirty traitor, too, but that's something I will never admit.

I didn't care about the bully's threats. I had been chosen by Susana. She'd asked me to keep her secret. Susana had a crush on me.

I'm really bad at keeping a secret. I need to let it out any way possible—just like Bernabé, Luisa's husband, who needs to let out gas when he comes home from work. I wanted to go to school wearing a big sign that said in capital letters:

SUSANA HAS A CRUSH ON ME

But I couldn't take the risk of telling just anyone. I thought my grandpa was the only person on the face of this Earth I could trust, and when we were in bed I told him the whole story, all the nitty and all the gritty. My grandpa put in his teeth to say, "That Susana is something else."

"Grandpa, I only have five euros in my pig. Can you loan me another five?"

And he gave them to me. Next, I did everything I could to make the hole in the knee of my sweatpants bigger, and after showing my mom and then lowering my head in shame so she could lecture me, I went with her to buy a new pair.

My mom found one of her awesome deals: for every three adult sweatsuits with Ninja Turtles on them that you buy, you get two kids' Ninja Turtle sweatsuits free. One for my mom, one for my dad, one for my grandpa, one for me, and one for the Bozo.

My mom smothers me and the Bozo with kisses when we're dressed alike. Don't ask me why. It's one of those unsolved mysteries of science.

For at least a week, I tried to talk as little as possible so that I wouldn't let out my terrible secret. It was actually easy, because Big Ears and Ozzy were really quiet, too.

Time dragged on till the next Monday, but Monday finally arrived, as it usually does in Spain and other European countries. In the afternoon, I washed my feet without my mom even having to yell at me. I brushed my teeth, even though I don't like to go overboard with cleaning. I heard my mom in the living room tell Luisa, "I don't know what's wrong with him: he's washing up."

"Let's hope you don't have to take him to see the psychologist again because he's going through another personality change," said Luisa to calm her down.

I took out my new sweatsuit from the drawer; I combed my hair with a Superman wave; I put on some of my dad's aftershave; I grabbed the envelope with the money; and I took one last look at myself in the mirror. I don't mean to brag or anything, but when I dress up, I look pretty sharp. I took a deep breath before coming out of the bathroom and heading toward the most important birthday party of my life.

Manolito Four-Eyes

My mom and Luisa, who were on the sofa, looked at me with a pretty worried look on their faces.

"Are you feeling all right, honey?"

"You want us to go with you?" asked Luisa.

Did I want them to come with me, they wanted to know?? Does someone go with Superman on his important missions? Does Zorro ever ask for help in times of need? Has Batman ever called on an army? Has Spider-Man ever demanded a ladder to climb up a wall?

This was a secret mission. Manolito needed no one.

Susana's mom, my future mother-in-law, opened the door for me.

"Hey, Manolito, nice to see you."

But when I walked into the living room, I knew I would have to share my mother-in-law and the One-and-Only Susana with Ozzy and Big Ears and Paquito Medina and Arturo Román and Oscar Mayer (not the hot dog man; this one's a kid in my class). . . . They were all there. We were all wearing the same sweatsuit, we all had the Superman wave. We all just stood there staring at each other.

Susana's mom broke the ice: "Well, kids, there are sandwiches on the table."

We started eating like we'd never eaten before: very politely. We sang "Happy Birthday" like we were the Vienna Boys' Choir.

"Are you having fun?" Susana's mom asked.

And we all nodded.

Her mom asked, "And . . . didn't anyone bring Little Susana a present?"

We all took out an envelope from our sweatsuits, and we put them on the table. Susana gathered them up quickly.

"Well, since we're all done, can we go to Hangman's Park?" said Arturo Román, who always says what nobody else dares to.

We threw ourselves at the door like madmen. We had to get out of that apartment where danger was lurking.

After a while, Susana came down and had the nerve to interrupt our bottle cap game. She's like that. Looking down at the ground, she said, "My mom told me to give you back your money, that you can't do that, and I look like a wheeler-dealer. You all have to buy me whatever you want."

"Why in the heck did you tell us not to tell anyone about the birthday party? We all ended up going anyway," said Ozzy.

"I told you to keep the money a secret, not the party, you stooges. You guys ruined it. I was going to buy an MP3 player with that money."

And she left. She's got quite a little attitude, that girl.

Since we're not really spiteful, we put all our money together, and Big Ears and I were in charge of going to Wal-Mart and getting the MP3 of her dreams. Our moms, who showed up in the same sweatsuit that was on sale, took us. This past Sunday, I went to buy tasty fried *churros* with my dad. Parents, sons and daughters, grand-parents, all of Carabanchel was wearing the same sweatsuit. That sweatsuit is like Susana: you think you're the only one in the world who's going to be sporting it, and then you gotta suck it up and deal with it because Carabanchel has turned into the hideout of the Ninja Turtles.

No matter how hard Ozzy tried, Susana wasn't his girl-friend, or Big Ears' girlfriend, or mine. Susana was all of Spain's girlfriend.

11

Supermanolito

My mom and Our Nosy Neighbor Luisa were psyched that Superman was on TV last Monday. Don't get me wrong: they're not Superman fanatics. They're not really into flying men, but when Superman's on TV, they can go out without having to worry about me and the Bozo, because they know we're gonna be glued to the sofa until *The End* comes up big on the screen.

Half an hour before my mom left, the apartment was filled with the sound of her heels on the hard floor and the smell of the perfume that my dad bought her to scare away all the men in the world. After a little while, Luisa came up to get her. Now there was double the heels and double the perfume. The Bozo said, "Baby smells stink."

When I saw that my mom and Luisa were dying laughing, I said, "If I'd been the one to make that comment instead of him, you guys would have killed me."

And my mom complained to Luisa that I was being a pain in the rump, that I bug my brother all day long, and that with brothers like me in the world there will always be civil war, and she ended her long speech, "Don't worry, because you can watch Superman by yourself. We're taking the baby with us, so he won't bother you anymore. It's hard to believe that he's your brother, the way you treat him."

At that moment, the Bozo made a humanitarian gesture that I will never forget: he took his pacifier out and said, "Baby wants with Manolito."

My mom stood there staring at us as if we were her worst enemy's kids.

"Let's go," she said to Luisa.

They slammed the door behind them, and the Bozo and I ran over to the window. We weren't going to say good-bye, yeah right; we were going to open it because we were about to choke to death with all that toxic perfume in the air.

I do not recommend getting into an elevator with Our Nosy Neighbor Luisa and her perfume. I'm saving that story line for when I'm a famous director of horror films: *The Mysterious Elevator Killer.* It'll be a blockbuster hit.

That's what was running through my head when the Superman song came on. We turned around and walked over to the sofa like we were possessed by a supernatural force. The Bozo buried his pacifier in the sugar bowl and he climbed on my lap. I stuffed a handful of Cocoa Krispies in my mouth and I thought, if it weren't for the fact that we have to share the same parents, the Bozo would be the best brother in the world. I didn't think about that for very long. Thinking about your family while you're watching Superman is pretty dumb.

We were halfway through the movie when, suddenly, the TV got all fuzzy. That's when we realized that the sky

was black and it was pouring. Then there was this loud thunder, the loudest one I've ever heard in my life on this planet, and our whole apartment shook. The Bozo's chin was trembling. When the Bozo's chin trembles it's because his heart is crying, not like when he cries just to be annoying. The TV went totally dead. Superman had abandoned us.

I swallowed hard and made a tough decision: I would be that older brother my mom had always dreamed about. I would be known as Manolito the Protector, Supermanolito. Now my mom would know what I was capable of. I would be the typical heroic kid.

I picked up my brother, cleared my throat like the tough guys in the movies, and said, "Do not fear, little one; it's just a little storm. Remember this: after a storm, comes a calm."

What a speech! It was so good, I impressed myself. Too bad it ended with this terrifying lightning bolt that lit up the living room, and thunder that made the walls of the García Moreno mansion shake. The Bozo, who at first after hearing my speech was all thoughtful, started crying again even louder (if that were possible).

The room was getting darker and darker, so I picked up the Bozo (all thirty-five pounds of him), and I went to turn on the light, but the light, just like Superman, had abandoned us.

It was becoming harder and harder to be Supermanolito, but I sat down on the sofa and dunked the

Bozo's pacifier in the sugar till the whole thing was covered and put it back in the Bozo's mouth, taking advantage of the fact that he had opened it to cry. As you can imagine, the whole scene, with the lightning, thunder, wind, and the Bozo's crying, looked like something out of *The Addams Family*. Even I, Supermanolito, that cold-blooded unwavering kid, was getting a little nervous. For a minute the Bozo stopped crying and he concentrated on the sugar, making his favorite noise, *smack-smack-smack-smack-smack.* . . .

Don't ask me what it means. Language experts have tried to decipher that strange word, but they haven't had any luck.

Water was coming in through the window, getting our beloved minibar wet. I thought, "This is how the Flood started." At least Noah had his whole family there, like some roosters, horses, elephants—you know, people he could turn to during difficult times in his life. If my apartment block flooded, I'd only have the Bozo. Why didn't my mom come back once and for all and save her children from this natural disaster? Was she still trying on bathing suits at Wal-Mart while her oldest son was left in charge of everything?

I got up to close the window, but there was this big gust of wind and the window slammed shut and the glass shattered. I wondered what Superman would have done at that scary moment. And what about you guys? What would you have done? You think you're so brave, huh? Supermanolito took his brother and the sugar bowl to an atomically safe refuge: his parents' closet. I closed the door from the inside and we stayed there, on the floor among all my mom's shoes (that didn't smell) and my dad's (that did).

We cried a little at first. It's a good thing that Supermanolito had been smart enough to take the sugar with him. We comforted ourselves with it—the Bozo used his pacifier and I used my finger—so much so that we must have fallen asleep.

After a while we heard the faint sound of heels, but I was really, really sleepy. Plus, I didn't dare go out because I was sure I was going to be in trouble. The Bozo woke up and I whispered to him, "Don't even think of talking." We stayed like that not just for a while, more like five whiles. We must have been there for days, months, even years. Suddenly, the door opened and we saw Luisa, who yelled, "Cata, they're here!"

My mom came running. She looked at us there on the floor between all the shoes, with the Bozo clinging to me like a leech. I was ready to hang my head in preparation for one of her historic lectures, but it was all for nothing. What happened next is . . . they took us out of the closet, and they gave us a glass of milk and some buns. My mom sat me on her lap and said, "Manolito, you're not going to tell Daddy you guys were home alone during the storm, right?"

Suddenly, a lightbulb came on in my head. I realized I had her where I wanted her, that if my dad found out about the fright we had, he would yell at her. "What should I do?" I thought, savoring the moment. . . .

"No, Mommy, I won't tell Daddy anything."

"You're my favorite son," she whispered in my ear.

And even though I knew it wasn't true, that she was just saying that to bribe me into not talking, because her favorite son (all of Spain knows it) is the Bozo, and even though I knew that sooner or later I would tell on my mom (I told you, I can't keep a secret), I sat there on her lap all through dinner.

What?! Supermanolito has his weaknesses, too.

12

Aunt Melitona

One day, Miss Asunción came into class carrying a huge cardboard box. As you can imagine, that made us pretty nervous.

"What's in the box?" asked Arturo Román, who always asks what's on all thirty of our minds.

Our Teach didn't say anything. She flashed a cruel smile at us and, very mysteriously, turned around to write something on the board.

While she was writing, all thirty of us kids walked slowly over toward the box, first without making a sound, and thirty seconds later like Madrid soccer fans, jumping all over each other. Ozzy had already climbed up on Miss Asunción's desk when she turned around and yelled,

"What are you doing? Go back to your seats, delinquents!"

We went back to our seats. You could hear the beating of our thirty little hearts from across the room. But surprisingly, Our Teach didn't keep on yelling at us. She smiled with her immense teeth and said, "From now on we're going to spend an hour every day rehearsing a song for the End of the Year Festival. I want your parents to be impressed. I want them to think, 'Wow, it doesn't look like my kid up there. It looks like a real person and not that delinquent who comes home from school every day kicking his lunch box.'"

That's what Miss Asunción thinks of us. Our Teach has one real virtue: sincerity.

When she finished insulting us, she opened the box and took out tambourines, a drum, and a glass bottle. Then she handed out the stuff. Ozzy, who's not shy, said, "Miss, if you let me have the drum I swear I'll be good for the next twenty-four days."

Our Teach accepts those kind of bribes because she knows he's a problematic kid. Not even a kid from the Chicago mafia can hold a candle to Ozzy. She gave me this funky glass bottle that was all sculpted and stuff, because I told her that Coke is my grandpa's favorite drink, and I play music with the empty bottle every day when the song comes on at the beginning of the news. That's a rotten lie: I don't use it to play music; I use it to make a tower for my Viking men to climb.

Once the instruments were handed out, Miss Asunción finished writing the song on the board. The song was called "Aunt Melitona," and it was about this lady who couldn't bake because she didn't have all the necessary ingredients.

Aunt Melitona can't bake at this hour.
She has no water, no salt, no flour
And the yeast she left in Pamplona;
How will she bake, dear Aunt Melitona?

The song is a lot longer than that; that's just the part that gets at the real heart of the matter.

During the next few days we rehearsed. Mustard (that's his real name, believe it or not) sang the first two lines because he's the shortest kid in my class; that's why I like him so much. If it weren't for Mustard, I'd be the shortest kid, so I'm eternally grateful to him for that. Sometimes I feel like his protector, even though Mustard doesn't know it and he doesn't need anyone to protect him. We call him the Atomic Ant because the guy's super fast; plus, he's a real good singer.

So anyway, Mustard sang the first two lines:

Aunt Melitona can't bake at this hour.
She has no water, no salt, no flour

And then we all joined in, singing the part about the yeast and playing our instruments; and, to be honest, once we all joined in you couldn't understand anything.

At first, we were really bad, but we didn't move from our places. Then, we were still really bad, but we were fighting, too. Ozzy threw one of his drumsticks at Big Ears because he said that Big Ears was playing the tambourine so loud that you couldn't hear his drum. Big Ears, who's a dirty traitor and on top of that has really fast reflexes, ducked, and the drumstick hit me in the glasses, and I dropped the bottle and the bottle broke.

That afternoon my grandpa had to drink four Cokes so I could take the bottles to school (I wanted three for backup). My grandpa will do anything for me. He had to drink them behind my mom's back, well aware of the fact that sooner or later he would be discovered, because my mom always counts how much Coke is left at the end of the day.

Miss Asunción took the drum away from Ozzy and gave it to Susana. She also took the tambourine away from Big Ears because the guy had gotten so excited that he had started whacking it on his knees and elbows, and Miss Asunción told him to save that monkey business for when he was in the high school band.

Our Teach showed the ones who sang the worst how to lip-sync, and the rest of us protested forcefully. We all wanted to lip-sync; that's what singers who reach the top do. Miss Asunción handed out the roles one more time. She said that from now on, yelling and protesting were not allowed.

"Any questions?"

Arturo Román, who's in his own little world, raised his hand:

"I don't get why the lady left the yeast in Pamplona. Isn't there anyone who can bring it to her in Madrid or who can send it by messenger? If someone sent it by FedEx the yeast would get there in less than twenty-four hours."

The bravest kids laughed out loud, and those of us who are cowards laughed on the inside because we know that Miss Asunción doesn't like those kinds of comments.

Our Teach sent Arturo Román outside for a while for being a smart aleck. She was wrong. He wasn't being a smart aleck; it's just that his brain should be donated to the Museum of Natural Science.

The next day, Miss Asunción decided to go on to the second part: the dancing. Some of us would sing, others would lip-sync, some would play instruments, and a couple would dance in the middle. Miss Asunción told us to start singing and that she would do a demonstration. Mustard stood up, filled his chest with air, and began:

Aunt Melitona can't bake at this hour.
She has no water, no salt, no flour

But he got an unexpected frog in his throat, and we all roared with laughter. Some kids fell on the ground. I resisted the urge because the four Cokes hadn't agreed with my grandpa the day before, and my mom told him he couldn't have any more for the rest of the week, and if I broke the bottles I wouldn't have anyone to drink another four for me.

"What happened, Mustard?" Our Teach asked, yelling over all the ruckus.

"I have a loogie in my throat, Miss Asunción," said

Mustard, staring at the ground. Once again everyone burst out laughing just as loud as before.

"It's not called a loogie, for the love of God!" yelled Miss Asunción.

"I don't know what else to call it," said Mustard, who was still staring at the ground.

"What you have is some phlegm. You guys don't even know how to talk. Go to the bathroom and clear your throat!" Mustard left and Our Teach turned around to tell us, "The rest of you, don't laugh because you're all the same: delinquents."

After three minutes, Mustard came back as red as a tomato and got into place. He took a deep breath, cleared his throat, and started again:

Aunt Melitona can't bake at this hour.
She has no water, no salt, no flour

And then we all yelled like crazy and banged on the instruments. Miss Asunción started dancing and hopping in the air. It looked like a weird rendition of this folk dance from the north of Spain called the *Jota*. We all started singing slower and slower because we were a little freaked out. We had never witnessed such a spectacle, with legs flying uncontrollably through the air. I personally had never seen her lift her feet off the ground. Except to walk, of course. Arturo Román, who was still outside, opened the door slowly and asked, "What is she doing?"

We didn't know what to say. Then, in one of those lethal hops, Our Teach's feet slipped out from under her, or at least they weren't on the ground when she was supposed to land on them, and she fell on her butt. We died laughing. Ozzy imitated the way she fell, and then we all did. All of a sudden, we heard Miss Asunción say in a very low voice, without getting up off the floor, "Go get the maintenance man."

It took the maintenance guy and three teachers to carry Miss Asunción because she's pretty fat. When we saw how they were putting her in the ambulance, we felt pretty bad.

Our Teach has been gone for two weeks now. Mr. Solís, the maintenance guy and bus driver, has been keeping an eye on us, and Miss Asunción sends homework from the hospital. Yeah, she broke her hip.

That afternoon my grandpa and Mr. Solís took us to see her. She was in a room with two ladies who were fat, too, but that was a coincidence. (It's not like in hospitals they put the fat ladies in separate rooms.)

We brought her some flowers and a box of chocolates that all us kids ate. (She might've had one, though.) Then we told her to close her eyes. When she opened them, we were all in our places, with our instruments, with Big Ears and Jessica the ex-Fat Fatty in the middle, our dance couple. Big Ears was voted by all the boys to be the one to dance, because he never falls. His ears help

him keep his balance. And Jessica the ex-Fat Fatty was voted by all the girls because she doesn't care if you see her underwear when she twirls around, and the other girls do.

My grandpa said, "One, two, three!"

Mustard, the Atomic Ant, cleared his throat to scare away all the terrible phlegm and started singing the story about Aunt Melitona. The rest of us followed, without hitting each other or yelling, without acting like we always do. Miss Asunción got teary-eyed. A whole bunch of people clapped for us: nurses, the other two fat ladies, and a stretcher-carrier guy. Mr. Solís lined us up so we could kiss Our Teach good-bye, and she said, "Well, delinquents, let's see how you behave while I'm gone."

And we left her there, alone. She reminded me of Aunt Melitona who must've been single like Miss Asunción, because if she had family she wouldn't have had to wait so many years for someone to send her the darn yeast from Pamplona. For once, Arturo Román was right.

13

The Return of Aunt Melitona

Miss Asunción came back. She was carrying a cane, and she walked through the halls of our school dragging her leg. That made her look pretty scary, like one of those humongous women in the movies who kidnap hundreds of innocent kids and dedicate their lives to threatening them with their canes, and then they laugh so hard the walls of their diabolic mansions shake.

Okay, I'm exaggerating a little bit; I'll admit it. The reality of it was pretty different. You couldn't hear Our Teach laugh because she was totally hoarse. Mr. Solís explained to us that in the hospital they had put this lethal tube down her throat so that she wouldn't suffocate when they were operating on her, and that had left her with no voice.

"After they took out the tube, did Miss Asunción spit blood?"

That was Big Ears, because he loves all that stuff about deadly diseases and operating rooms. For our last essay, Miss Asunción let us write about whatever we wanted, and Big Ears wrote about an autopsy. The person telling the story was the dead guy. When he started reading it out loud in front of the class, Arturo Román cried because he was so scared. Big Ears was sent straight to the school psychologist so drastic measures could be taken. He's still in therapy as we speak.

So, back to what I was saying, that Miss Asunción came back mute, but real excited to see us. I'm sure she didn't want to miss the last month of school because that's when she gives out grades. She wouldn't have been happy if someone else had gotten to write the Fs on our report cards. That's her hobby. Some people like soccer, some like going to the movies, Our Teach likes writing Fs, even though she says that in today's world you're not allowed to put F and you have to write "not satisfactory." Well, she just has to make do with that. It's better than nothing.

She opened the door to the classroom and flashed us a huge smile with those big teeth. She limped over to the board and wrote:

How's it going, delinquents?

And we all said:

"Good, Miss Asunción!"

And she erased her first note and wrote:

This week, since I can't yell, I'm going to give you work to do in class.

After she wrote that, she filled up the board with ruthless math problems.

We were all a little in shock. We thought her return was going to be a lot more emotional, and that, with the whole reuniting thing, we were gonna spend the last month of school just hanging out and talking about our feelings. But no, Miss Asunción doesn't have any feelings.

We started doing the problems and the noise level slowly started rising. It always begins as just a little murmur and then gets louder and louder till Miss Asunción launches her first warning: "I'm going to start taking off points!"

The murmur dies down and then very slowly starts up again till it gets to the same level as before, and then Our Teach yells:

"Arturo Román, go out in the hallway! Ozzy, I'm taking off a point! Manolito, this is the last time I'm going to warn you! Mustard, don't sing while you're counting! Big Ears, stop telling Manolito about *Friday the 13th*; then his mom comes and says he has bad dreams! Susana, if you pull on Jessica's desk again I'm going to tell your grandma when she comes to get you! Everyone be quiet now!"

That's how we spend most of our days. That's our life. But, of course, the day Miss Asunción came to school with no voice was different. No yelling from Our Teach, and we need that yelling. So when the noise level started getting louder and louder, and Miss Asunción put her first warning on the board, everyone looked at it, but without really taking it seriously; because no matter how you look at it, yelling in writing is just not the same as yelling out loud, live and unplugged. Ten minutes later, I was whispering in Big Ears' ear, and not because I was trying to be discreet. It was so loud in the class that we couldn't hear each other, despite the fact that we were sitting right next to each other. We were having such a blast that we didn't see the principal come in. He was standing in the middle of the room.

"Quiet, I said!" screamed the principal, and we all sat there like we never do: totally quiet. "Can't you see the board?"

Uh, no, we hadn't seen it till right then. The board was full of warnings, threats, minus points, insults. . . . Nobody had paid any attention to Miss Asunción; so, totally at her wits' ends with us out-of-control kids, she had gone home and left us this last note:

Good-bye, delinquents. You haven't seen the last of me.

The next day when we got to school, we were all pretty scared, and we were making bets about what was going to happen. Was she going to hand out Fs? Was she going to send a letter to our parents? Was she going to suspend us all from school?

None of that happened. Miss Asunción came into class, as if second chances were possible in life, smiling with her big teeth and dragging her leg over to the board. She wrote:

How's it going, delinquents?

We all answered, pretty shocked:

"Good, Miss Asunción."

And she kept writing, like one of those bad dreams that you have three nights in a row.

This week, since I can't yell, I'm going to give you work to do in class.

She started writing more of those darn division problems and the famous murmur started up once again, because we're not real big on learning from experience. We're that animal that trips over the same stone during its whole existence. Even if there are other stones even bigger and in worse places, we always trip on the same one. Something in our brain just doesn't work.

When the murmur turned into yelling, Miss Asunción went to the middle of the room and . . .

We almost jumped right out of our seats. We heard this really loud whistle, a whistle that could have been from the Madrid soccer stadium, a whistle that could lead a herd of

✿ the same stone

elephants from one side of the African continent to the other.

Miss Asunción had gone out and bought a whistle, and she smiled all happy with our reaction when she blew it for the first time. Everybody shut up right away. We got back to work with our hearts in our mouths.

And that's how the worst days of our lives began. Miss Asunción was so excited with the results of her super-whistle that she started acting like a referee and a traffic guard. It was a mix of the two professions. She directed us out to the playground and back into the classroom, waving her arms like a guard. During class, she took out yellow cards, like a referee. We didn't take our eye off her because we didn't want her to catch us off guard. She enjoyed coming up behind us and blowing the whistle. We almost died of a heart attack every time she did it. Then she'd laugh silently. I still have that picture in my mind of Our Teach's silent laughter. I'm saving it for my worst nightmares.

That's when Ozzy had a great idea that would change the course of history forever. We were on the playground, over in the corner, talking real quiet because we didn't dare yell, even outside, when Ozzy said, "Have you guys noticed that during recess she leaves the whistle on her desk? Well tomorrow, when she goes to eat her sandwich in the teacher's lounge, I'm going to put an end to this matter."

"Are you really going to take her whistle away?" asked Big Ears.

"I don't have to get my hands dirty stealing. Just trust me."

The next day, when the bell rang, instead of throwing ourselves at the door like we always do, we just kinda hung around till Miss Asunción went out with her humongous sandwich to the teacher's lounge.

"Arturo, keep a lookout at the door, and the rest of you, form a circle around me. If Miss Asunción comes back, we'll tell her we're playing 'telephone.'"

We formed a circle around Ozzy. It was Paquito Medina, me, and Big Ears. Ozzy took out a super-duper multipurpose nailclipper and, with the blade, he sliced open Miss Asunción's whistle where it was glued shut. He took out the pea from inside and then took out a little bottle of glue from his other pocket and glued the two parts of the whistle back together again so it looked just like before. Just like before . . . at first glance. He put the whistle back on Miss Asunción's desk.

When the bell rang at the end of recess, I started getting the giggles because I was so nervous, but Ozzy threatened to kick us if we didn't act natural—like the same kids we always are, with all of our imperfections and all of our . . . imperfections.

Our Teach wrote some sentences on the board. She likes it when we say which word is the verb and which word is the subject. It's this whim she's had since the school year began.

We started writing and talking. I don't know why that

happens. You start doing schoolwork, and you immediately feel like talking to anyone about anything, from endangered species to the hole in the ozone layer or the hole you have in your sock. Scientists from all over the world have tried to figure out why all the kids on this planet have the same reaction, but they've had to acknowledge that science doesn't have answers for everything.

We started talking in a normal tone, like always, then we started yelling, like always, but those of us who were in on the whole scheme were talking normally out of one side of our mouths, and, out of the other side, we were laughing. I was savoring that historic moment, enjoying every second. Our Teach went to the middle of the room and put the whistle up to her mouth and blew with all her might, and when she heard no sound come from her beloved whistle, she stared at it with indignation, like the whistle had committed some kind of crime or serious offense—like the whistle were one of us.

The whole class burst out laughing. Ozzy got a few pats on the back and he stood up to take a bow, like an important musician after a masterful performance. Miss Asunción watched us with one eyebrow raised, her face getting redder and redder, while we were talking about what we had just seen.

"IT'S NOT FUNNY!!!!!!!!"

We'd never heard Miss Asunción scream like that. And, man, have I heard her scream. Now we were the ones who were totally silent. Dead silent. We all wanted to pull our

shirt collars up real high and hide our heads like turtles. That's what we do when we're getting chewed out. How had Miss Asunción managed to get her voice back, just like that?

We were still getting over our hearts racing at a thousand beats a minute when the principal opened the door and, panting, said, "Asunción, what's going on?"

Miss Asunción touched her throat, swallowed, and said, surprising herself, "I don't know . . . since I hadn't talked in a week, I didn't realize I had my voice back."

"Do you think you could yell at them without making the walls shake?"

"Yes, of course. It's just that they took the pea out of my whistle and . . ."

Man, Our Teach is smart. She looked at each one of us, but her gaze stopped at Ozzy.

"Ozzy, you're going to put it back right now, and if you can't do it, you're going to have to buy me a new one."

Miss Asunción is a psychic. Ozzy walked over to get the whistle with his head down and then went over to her desk to fix it.

Before leaving, the principal cleared his throat and said to Miss Asunción very politely, "I think it's a good idea if the young man fixes it, but . . . well, now that your voice is back, I think the school could get back to normal, if you stopped using the whistle. Maybe, some day, when we go camping, you can use it again."

"Sure," said Miss Asunción, not really knowing what to say.

Ozzy fixed the whistle. Miss Asunción looked at it nostalgically and with a little grin said, "Well, Ozzy, since you know this mechanism better than anyone, and I can't use it anymore, you better keep it. But just remember: you can't blow it at school."

Ozzy took the gift and, turning bright red, mumbled a barely audible "thanks." Then, on the way home, he wouldn't stop bragging about how Miss Asunción had given it to him as a gift because he knew the mechanism better than anyone.

"Now we're going to have to put up with Ozzy and his stupid whistle," I said secretly to Big Ears.

"With that gross noise it makes," Big Ears said to me, also secretly.

But this story doesn't end with some poor kids having to put up with a pain in a butt who won't stop bragging about a whistle his teacher gave him. This story ends with five kids (six with the Bozo) blowing whistles as hard as they can in Hangman's Park and watching how old men, women, and children run away terrified—because my grandpa and Ozzy's grandpa, when they realized that we were all jealous of the famous disgusting whistle, thought the only solution was to buy each one of us our own whistle. And, the truth is, when your own lungs are producing that diabolical noise, it sounds different; it sounds—how can I describe it . . . like little celestial angels singing.

The little angels are—you guessed it—us.

14

The Filthy Feet Gang

That historic Saturday afternoon, we ate six bags of potato chips, two bags of Cheetos, two bags of pork rinds, and six bags of Fritos. We washed it all down with Coke from last year's vintage, and we watched a movie about some kids who lived next to a cliff and had a gang that solved criminal cases and had a secret word and a hideout and a dog that did everything except talk.

We were at Big Ears' house, lying on the couch, from left to right: Arturo Román, me, Big Ears, and Paquito Medina, and in two armchairs, Ozzy and the Bozo.

Ozzy was making jokes about those kids, and we were laughing at their secret word and their secret meetings. We were in the middle of a laughing fit, jumping on top of each other, having a ball making fun of those kids, when Ozzy said, "Let's form a gang, too."

Five minutes later we were sitting there thinking of names, secret words, and secret meeting places. You're probably wondering what we were doing imitating the very kids we had been making fun of. It's a good question, and it really only has one answer: we can't be trusted. Don't ever place your trust in us.

From the moment our gang was formed, the indisputable leader was Ozzy—something we've known from the beginning of time, gang or no gang. Then we had to think of a name, and I don't mean to blow my own horn or anything, but I was the one who thought of this: "Since Miss Asunción makes us take a shower every day so she doesn't die of asphyxiation, we could call ourselves the Filthy Feet Gang and we could honor our name by not washing our feet." Saying that, I felt like a savage.

"*You* can honor our name, because ever since Miss Asunción said we smelled putrid, my mom doesn't let me leave the house unless I scrub my whole body with one of those scrubbers," said Big Ears.

"Me, either," said Paquito Medina.

The cruel reality of things was spoiling my great idea.

"Then we can call ourselves the Clean Feet Gang," Big Ears piped up.

We looked at him from head to toe. The Clean Feet Gang?! No respectable gang could ever be called Clean Feet. Desolation filled Big Ears' living room.

"Well, we can just do our missions on the weekends, when we can be true Filthy Feet," said Ozzy, taking off his shoes and stomping on the floor.

∽ᴏᴏ

That was the beginning of the Filthy Feet, that mythical gang from Carabanchel that acted only on Saturdays and Sundays, whose goal in life was to fight against evil, who didn't have a movie star dog but settled for Miss Bonnie, Our Nosy Neighbor Luisa's dog (who had to be carried because she wasn't a real action dog), and who didn't have a hideout but established Hangman's Tree as a meeting point.

Members of the Filthy Feet had to walk out of their homes before their moms broke the spell with the power of water and soap. Once on the street, the Filthy Feet took their shoes off and walked all over till their feet were black. The Filthy Feet had a treasurer, whose name was Manolito Four-Eyes. They named this guy treasurer because he was a trustworthy guy and because he had an empty piggy bank to put the gang's money in. The Filthy Feet's money was used only for special missions.

The first special mission proposed by the leader of the Filthy Feet was throwing all the Tech guys out of Hangman's Park, because they had taken it over as a soccer field, and they didn't let the old people and the little kids enjoy the magnificent facilities the park had to offer (the magnificent facilities include a bench, two swings, dirt, and the actual Hangman's Tree). When the leader asked for volunteers to carry out such a risky mission, nobody raised their hand. Why? Because Filthy Feet love life too much to face guys who wear a size-11 shoe. The leader (Ozzy) said that he didn't care if there were volunteers or not, because we were going in by force.

That fateful Sunday, the Filthy Feet left their homes, took off their shoes in the park, and sat down to wait for the Tech School gang to arrive.

After forty-five minutes, they showed up. They didn't even look at us. They started to kick the ball around like a bunch of animals. Ozzy gave us the signal and, with fear in our bones, we went out into the ring.

We stood in the middle of the park so they couldn't play. There we were, barefoot: Paquito Medina, Arturo Román, Big Ears, Ozzy, Manolito, and the Bozo. The Filthy Feet.

"Get out of the way, midgets!" yelled one of the Tech guys.

But since we didn't budge, they kept playing over our heads. The ball was flying over my thoughts. For a moment, I felt like one of those poor pins you gotta bump off when you go to the bowling alley. I thought about my glasses, about how some hadn't lasted me very long. The only thing you could hear was the fast-paced *smack-smack-smack-smack* of the Bozo sucking on his pacifier (you could tell he was nervous) and the ball being kicked around. I closed my eyes because I was imagining that, from one minute to the next, that ball was going to plow

me over, and I didn't want to see it. I'm not a masochistic kid. But when I opened my eyes, I wasn't lying on the ground. . . .

A new phenomenon had occurred in Carabanchel. For the first time in our lives I wasn't the one hurt; it was Ozzy who was covering his face with his hand.

"It's you guys's fault for being annoying," said one of the Tech guys.

The Filthy Feet took their leader, who couldn't open his right eye, off the field. As soon as we dragged the injured man off, the Tech guys kept on playing as if nothing had happened. It was our first casualty in the gang and the last one, because our leader decided that these kinds of secret missions were stupid and that we couldn't care less about the old people and the kids having peaceful afternoons in the park.

Now what were we going to dedicate our funds and energy to?

"We'll be a cultural organization," said Ozzy.

So we decided that the money we had in the piggy bank would be used to fund activities like visiting Mr. Mariano's stand, filling up a bag with candy, and watching a movie at Big Ears' house.

We went right back to normal, but with a treasurer. Well, it was exciting being part of the Filthy Feet Cultural Association and being able to share our money with our best friends. On Saturdays we would go over to Big Ears' house, take off our shoes and watch a movie, and we'd finish off all our candy stock and Big Ears' mom's stock, too. (Big Ears' mom is a mom right out of a family movie.) Then, later on, after the Tech guys had finished their game, we'd go down to Hangman's Park, and there we'd pretend we were the characters in a movie. If we'd watched *Robin Hood*, we were Robin; if we'd watched *Batman*, we were Batman; if we'd watched *The Three Musketeers*, we were the Three Musketeers (Ozzy always had to be D'Artagnan. I had to settle for whatever they threw my way. Once, I had to play a dog.)

During the third week of the Filthy Feet Cultural Association, a strange thing began happening: we were putting more and more money in the Association's account, but there was less and less when we went to cash in. I had managed to hide the losses by adding some money from my own pocket, but the pig was running dry.

I showed up all sweaty to one of our sessions at Big Ears' house. The numbers weren't matching up, and I was fearing expulsion. We could barely buy anything, but I got out of trouble with the boss, because the Bozo shared his bag of candy with everybody. It was a huge bag. The Bozo was gaining popularity while I was losing it. He was becoming Ozzy's little favorite. That was terrible—like having the enemy at home.

"What are you doing with our money, Manolito?" yelled Ozzy.

"Yeah! What are you doing with it?" yelled my best friends, forming a circle around me.

I was about to be court-martialed when the Bozo piped up, "Baby buys with pig."

That said, and as if it was the most normal thing in the world, he took out a ton of coins from his pocket and put them in Ozzy's hand with a huge ear-to-ear smile (and his ears are pretty far apart). The Bozo had been opening the piggy bank's tummy the whole time, buying stuff, and then giving us presents with our own money.

We ate the rest of it; we watched a movie; and we dissolved the Association. We could do the same thing without any association. After all, it was always the same group of kids, playing the same thing, and eating the same junk. The difference was that now each of us had our own money again, so there were no outstanding debts to be paid. Filthy Feet would be no more.

That afternoon, when I got home, my mom erased the last trace of the Association when she put my feet under the faucet. One thing was for sure: if any of us were cold-blooded enough to lead an organized gang it was . . . the Bozo.

15

Miss Bonnie

When Our Nosy Neighbor Luisa asked my mom if we could keep Miss Bonnie one weekend, the Bozo and I were so crazy excited that we got up on top of the minibar.

Miss Bonnie is Luisa's dog. It's not a purebred; it's a cross, a cross between mutts that were found on the street; that's why Miss Bonnie is kind of weird-looking. She's got a fat head and a fat body, but she has skinny legs, like a ballet dancer. She has the same body type as Luisa, all of Carabanchel agrees. Even though my grandpa says Miss Bonnie's probably so fat because she lives like a duchess: she eats only steak and bonbons.

It must be true what they say about dogs looking like their owners. I once dreamed that I saw Luisa and Miss Bonnie playing in Hangman's Park, and instead of her own head, Luisa had Miss Bonnie's head, and Miss Bonnie had Luisa's head. Well, I was talking to them, and the whole time I didn't notice anything weird, but then suddenly it dawned on me and I asked Luisa, "What happened to your head?"

And Luisa, with her dog face, responded, "I never said anything because I was embarrassed, but I'm not entirely human. I'm a mutt."

Then Luisa starting barking and growling like she wanted to attack me, and I woke up from that terrible nightmare all upset and sweaty.

Since then, every time I ring Luisa's bell, while I'm waiting for her to open the door, I feel a shiver all the way up my spine.

So, yeah, you could say that Miss Bonnie hasn't been blessed by Mother Nature. She's ugly, but we love her a lot anyway. When we run into her on the stairs, she rolls over on the ground with her legs in the air so we can scratch her tummy, and it takes her a while to turn back over and get up because she's so fat and old. Luisa says the poor thing isn't able to do what she used to.

One day, Luisa and my mom got mad at each other over Miss Bonnie. It was because they caught the Bozo giving Miss Bonnie his pacifier to suck on. It wasn't the first time he'd done it; they've been sharing a pacifier for a long time, but moms are always the last ones to find out about their children's vices. Luisa snatched the pacifier from Miss Bonnie's mouth and said to the Bozo, "Don't do that again. The last thing I need is for you to give Miss Bonnie the snots!"

My mom picked up the Bozo, smothering him with her arms, and answered, "You got it backward, honey; Miss Bonnie's the one who's going to give my baby the snots."

I didn't say anything because there are times in your life when you're taking a big risk by talking, but it was clear that Luisa was right. The Bozo couldn't give Miss Bonnie the snots because calling those nasty leeches that come out of the Bozo's nose "the snots" is an understatement. The Bozo could give her *mucus hypersecretionus*. (Too bad no one is interested in buying his snot production because we'd be millionaires.)

My mom walked out and slammed the door behind her, but she wasn't mad for long because, half an hour later, she went down to ask her dear neighbor if she would mind watching us while she went to the store. Luisa whispered to the Bozo, "If Miss Bonnie gets sick from your pacifier, I'm going to give candy only to Manolito from now on."

The Bozo nodded, like he agreed. I know it's a tactic he uses so they don't lecture him, and then he just keeps doing his own thing. He's a rebellious kid.

So anyway, as I was saying, Luisa asked my mom to

watch Miss Bonnie for the weekend, and my mom said, "Of course, that's what friends are for." Even though later, my mom complained that Miss Bonnie had messed up her finances for the weekend because, like I said before, Miss Bonnie doesn't eat just any old thing that we eat at the García Moreno residence. Miss Bonnie has exquisite taste, even more exquisite than the Queen of Spain's.

ᗒᗕ

On Friday night, Miss Bonnie arrived. She brought her bone, her Smurf doll (that she also shares with the Bozo), and her crib. After my mom went to bed, I put Miss Bonnie up on our bed, down by our feet, but Miss Bonnie wasn't about to settle for that. When we woke up the next morning, we saw she had gotten right in the middle between me and my grandpa and had put her head on the pillow. After a while, the Bozo came in, like he does every

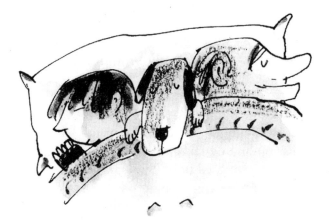

Saturday morning, and he started jumping on our heads. Miss Bonnie started barking, and we ended up pushing my grandpa onto the floor. If you'd been there, you'd know what it means to die laughing. But you missed it. Too bad.

My mom came in to hand out lectures. She was so upset she was waving her hands, and she accidentally whacked my grandpa in the head and he yelled, "Help! My family is trying to kill me before I even have breakfast!"

That's what Saturday mornings are like at the García Moreno residence: wild.

Me and the Bozo inhaled our breakfast so that we could go walk Miss Bonnie. While we were going down the stairs, we fought over who got to carry the leash.

"Take turns carrying it!" my mom yelled from above. "Don't take advantage of your brother, Manolito. He's little!"

Did she just say don't take advantage of the Bozo? That's impossible. If you say "no" to him, he has a fit in the middle of the street and you're done for. All the neighbors come to the window and scream down at me:

"Can't you see he's little, Manolito?"

"You should be ashamed of yourself, making a little boy cry like that."

That little boy was born to dominate me.

When we got to Hangman's Park, we let Miss Bonnie go. We threw sticks to play catch with her, like Lassie and other famous dog movie stars do. But Miss Bonnie climbed up on the bench as best she could and sat down next to us. I must say, she did watch very attentively while we threw sticks. She's a very observant dog. Me and the Bozo were getting bored playing with such a lazy dog, so we went over to the swings. I was pushing the Bozo on the swing with all my might. When the Bozo was up real high, and it looked like he was going to go all the way around, I yelled, "Danger!"

And the Bozo laughed real hard. He laughed so hard, he started choking and coughing brutally, so I had to sit him down on the bench. Man, this kid gives me a lot of problems. I whacked him hard on the back a few times so his saliva would go down the right tube when, suddenly, we realized that . . . Miss Bonnie was gone!

We yelled, "Miss Bonnie, Miss Bonnie!" We left the park and went to the Carabanchel jail and asked a guy there—who must've been a prisoner who had just been released after serving a forty-year-and-one-day sentence— if he'd seen Miss Bonnie. He hadn't. Ms. Porfiria, the storeowner, hadn't seen her, either, or Mr. Mariano, who sells candy and munchies.

Nobody had seen Miss Bonnie.

Our Nosy Neighbor Luisa was going to kill us—and what would become of such an observant and fat dog, all alone out on the streets and without a home? I started crying, and the Bozo tried to console me by offering me his pacifier. Even though I didn't put it in my mouth (three people sharing the same pacifier seems a bit much), I appreciated the gesture. I know it's a big deal for him.

With tears in our eyes, we walked into Stumbles, which is where my grandpa has breakfast on Saturdays. He has a decaf coffee and shrimp. That's when I saw

something that I will always remember as long as I live—unless I forget, of course. I couldn't believe what my glasses were seeing: Miss Bonnie was sitting on a chair, sharing a table with my grandpa. My grandpa was peeling shrimp, and Miss Bonnie was swallowing them whole.

"Is the Duchess here smart or what? She followed the scent of the shrimp. That's what I call following a trail!"

The Bozo and I sat down, too. We ordered a milkshake and more shrimp and French fries and olives and pork rinds, and Miss Bonnie tried it all, but she liked the shrimp best.

Later, my mom yelled at my grandpa because that Saturday we didn't eat the stew she'd made for lunch. The only one who kept eating was Miss Bonnie, and then, with her stomach all full of stew, she rolled over into the "scratch my tummy" position.

When Luisa came to get her on Sunday, Miss Bonnie said good-bye to us with tears in her eyes. Okay, I'm lying. The only ones who had tears in their eyes were me, my grandpa, and the Bozo.

16

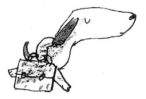

Miss Bonnie Goes to School

My grandpa says my mom makes such a big fuss every morning when I'm about to leave that it seems like I'm going off to America instead of going to school. My mom gives me a bunch of kisses on the landing that you can hear in all of Carabanchel, which just wipe me out. Then she takes out a comb from her bathrobe pocket and combs my hair again. Then the Bozo starts crying, because he's one of those kids who can't stand being separated from me (that's understandable). Then I have to hug him, and he leaves boogers on my shirt, and my mom goes to get a rag from the kitchen to wipe them off. Then she combs my hair again and suddenly for no reason, my mom, that nice affectionate lady, transforms into this hysterical lady and yells right in my inner ear, "Can't you see you're going to be late for school?"

While I'm going down the stairs, I hear the Bozo's howling. The man who lives on the fourth floor, who can't stand any ruckus, screams down like a madman, "Why doesn't somebody dip that kid's pacifier in chloroform!"

Our Nosy Neighbor Luisa comes out on a rampage and, while still putting on her bathrobe, yells up from the second floor, "If it bothers you that the little angel cries, why don't you go live in another building, or another neighborhood, or another country!"

I run out the front door because I hate violence, but the thing doesn't end there. When I turn the corner I hear, "Manolito!"

It's my mom. Again.

"You forgot your snack! Do I have to think of everything?"

With all that kissing, I forget my snack almost every day, so my mom bought an amazing rope to tie the snack to, and she lowers it down from the window.

"What it is?"

"Bologna sandwich."

It's always a bologna sandwich. As far back as I can remember, every day I've always had a bologna sandwich for a snack.

But then, Luisa opens the door and comes out with her pink fuchsia sweatsuit on and her mysterious smile, and Miss Bonnie appears between her legs, wagging her tail and with the same mysterious smile. I told you: they look like sisters. Luisa takes a peanut candy bar out of her pocket. "Here you go, Manolito, so you don't have the taste of bologna in your mouth."

I give Luisa five kisses, because I know that's how to make sure I get another candy bar the next day. I'm an affectionate little kiss-up. When Miss Bonnie sees us hug on the street, she gets right in the middle because she's jealous.

This happens every day (with some variations, of course). Sometimes Luisa wears a pink sweatsuit and other days a purple one. Sometimes my mom ties the sandwich to the rope. Other times, if it's real late and there's no time, she throws it down and it does a "free fall," and if we're lucky, it falls on some guy's head that's passing by, and the dying man starts screaming and holding his bloody head (I'm exaggerating a little here), and all the ladies on my block look out the window, and Miss Bonnie barks because Miss Bonnie's the same as me. She's against violence.

Yesterday, something happened that had never happened before. After Luisa gave me the candy bar, I couldn't resist the urge to sink my teeth into it, so I opened it and took a bite. I had to stop and close my eyes so I could enjoy that moment of pure bliss. I think I was about to levitate. Then, Miss Bonnie, who was having her first pee of the day by Hangman's Tree, came running over all excited and stopped in front of me.

"I'm not going to give you any, Miss Bonnie; you're too fat."

But Miss Bonnie kept staring at me, and she licked her snout and looked at me all sad. I don't know if a dog has ever looked at you like that, but if it didn't break your heart into five different chunks, you're not human. I broke off a little piece of peanut and gave it to her, and I started walking, because I was going to be late. When I got to the corner, I saw that Miss Bonnie was following me.

"Go home to Luisa, Miss Bonnie. I'm going to school."

I gave her another piece and said, "That's it; no more; good-bye."

I kept walking. I met up with Big Ears, and he put his arm around me. I thought, "Nothing beats friendship." But this thought didn't last because I realized Big Ears had put his arm around me to be closer to the candy bar. That's life for you: one big disappointment. Since I'm a softie, I gave him a piece, and he said, "Why don't you give Miss Bonnie a little?"

Miss Bonnie! She was still following me. I gave her the last chunk, and at the front gate of the school, I had a heart to heart with her, a man-to-dog talk. "Miss Bonnie, wake up; dogs don't go to school. If I could, I would go home and curl up on a pillow like you. Miss Bonnie, go. I promise you, this place is a bore galore."

But Miss Bonnie is a little mutt who knows what she wants. Without batting an eyelash, she followed me and Big Ears up the stairs. Since it was really late, there was no one else around. When we got to our classroom door, Big Ears said, "I'll go in first and while I'm making up some excuse, you can sneak in with Miss Bonnie."

And that's what we did. While Big Ears was telling Miss Asunción one of his incredible stories (last time he told her he'd saved an old crippled man from being run over by a truck), I went over to my desk, followed by Miss Bonnie, who was walking along the desks so that everyone would pat her. What a flirt.

We made her a little crib with all our backpacks over in the corner, and I gave her my bologna sandwich so she'd be quiet. She ate it and fell asleep. Our Teach noticed we were acting a little weird and said, "Don't forget that there are still three weeks left in the school year, so I don't want anyone to think they're already on vacation. I haven't made out your report cards yet."

We all shut up like the living dead. Then, during this total silence, there was a terrifying bark. Just one bark: "Woof!"

Miss Asunción had woken up Miss Bonnie with her yelling, and Miss Bonnie doesn't take that well. Like I said before: Miss Bonnie is a pacifist dog.

Our Teach took off her reading glasses and put on her distance glasses and looked over at the corner where Miss Bonnie was protesting. We thought her eyes were going to pop out of their sockets.

"What is *that* doing here?"

Silence.

"Who brought that rodent in here?"

(I'll admit it: I thought about not saying anything.)

"I didn't want to bring her, Miss Asunción—she followed me!"

"Get her out of here! God knows if she has fleas, ticks, some kind of fungus. . . ."

The door opened, and in walked the pink fuchsia sweatsuit, and in it was Luisa. She was clearly upset. She didn't say hi; she just threw herself at Miss Asunción and said, "Is my Bonnie here? Mr. Solís said that he saw her following Manolito."

Miss Bonnie ran over to Luisa, wagging her tail. Luisa hugged Our Teach and said, "Miss Asunción, thank you so much for taking care of her for me. Carabanchel can be proud to have a teacher like you who teaches her students to be kind to all living creatures."

Miss Asunción said thank you and that, for her, all living creatures were a divine blessing (I don't know if ticks were included in that). We all gave Miss Asunción a round

of applause. When school's almost over, we kiss-up more than ever.

Miss Bonnie barked because she realized she was not the center of attention anymore. And I wanted to bark, too, because everyone had forgotten that I was the real guilty one in this whole story. Miss Bonnie left, wagging her tail. Her pillow was waiting for her, that old pillow where she spends most of her life. What was waiting for me was four hours of sitting at my desk, pretending to be an A student, trying desperately to change what was already certain: my F in math.

17

A Little White Lie

The only bad thing about summer vacation is that with summer vacation come report cards. It would be so nice if one fine day in June, your teacher said to you, "Well, kids, school's almost out for the summer. Rest. Have fun. You deserve it for putting up with this torture we call school for a whole year. In the name of this institution, I apologize for what we've put you through."

That would be a gesture that we would never forget and that we would tell our kids about at holiday time. How nice it would be if the world was like I picture it. But no, what Miss Asunción said was, "All right, delinquents. The day after tomorrow you'll be getting your grades. There will be no surprises for anyone because each and every one of you knows very well . . . what you deserve."

Having said that, she flashed us one of her special smiles—specifically, that smile that's meant to make our blood run cold.

"Ha!" said Ozzy when we walked out. "Fs don't bother me at all. My mom's real happy with me because this year I haven't gotten a letter from the principal expelling me from school, so she tells the neighbors, 'Ozzy is going to be the surprise of the neighborhood; you wait and see. I wouldn't be surprised if he ends up being bishop of Carabanchel because, you wouldn't know it, but my little Ozzy's a sweetheart—a bit of a brute and a hooligan, but a sweetheart. I'm his mom; I should know.'"

"Report cards aren't any fun for me," said Paquito Medina. "My mom called my grandparents yesterday to tell them, 'I don't even need to see Paquito's report card. I know it's going to be like every other year: straight As.' So, since she doesn't need to see it, I might not even come pick it up."

Paquito Medina wishes he could be like me, an ordinary kid, and I wish I could be like Paquito Medina, a model kid. Maybe in the future, scientists will invent a machine so that unhappy kids can trade brains, but I'm afraid it will be too late for Paquito Medina and me.

Big Ears talked about his grades like it was a roll of the dice: "I don't know if I'm going to get two Fs, three Fs, or one F. . . . Of course, I could get four," he said, thinking out loud. "I guess that adds a little bit of excitement to the whole thing. One thing's for sure: my mom told me not to get upset, whatever it is, and my dad told me we'd get a tutor and a twenty-four-hour on-call psychologist so that I have everything I need this summer." He's a lost cause.

All my friends were making bets about how good or bad their report cards were going to be. I don't understand it. I knew perfectly well what I was going to get. The only thing that could save me now would be for Miss Asunción to grant me a last minute pardon and turn that F she was going to give me into a compassionate C by chopping off the lower branch and reattaching it at the bottom (because I don't think she would have the fantastic idea of drawing a diagonal branch on the right-hand side of it and making it into an A).

The morning I had to go get my report card, the Bozo got sick, so my grandpa had to take me to school. At least I had that going for me, although it was not going to help much, given the great misfortune that awaited me. I figured the worst thing about getting an F is having to listen to the conversation that goes on over your head between your teacher and your mom about what a stooge you are. Answer me this: what look should you have on your face when two women are having a grand old time tearing you apart right in front of you?

When we got to school, Big Ears, Ozzy, Susana, Paquito Medina, Arturo Román, and some other kids you don't know were already waiting on the bench in the hallway. My grandpa asked Susana's grandma if she was the last person in line, like he was at the deli. The difference, of course, was that we kids were going to be the lunch meat here.

It was Big Ears' turn, but he didn't go in, just his mom.

"The whole report card ritual is just not my thing," he explained to my grandpa.

This guy, I tell you. He's so cheeky, he could be a blowfish. If we caught him, we'd have to throw him back.

Finally Big Ears' mom came out and said to him in a sweet voice, "Well, honey, we're going to have to get you two on-call psychologists instead of one because you failed three subjects."

What do you think Big Ears said? What do you think was the only sentence that came out of his mouth at that awkward moment?

"And how many subjects are there?" he asked, really interested.

Sometimes I wonder if he knows what grade he's in.

"Seven, honey," answered his mom, looking like she wanted to cry. She put her hand on his shoulder and went to leave, but before she did, she looked at me and said, "Well, Manolito, let me know how it goes. I hope you're luckier than your friend," and she stroked my hair a little.

I don't know if I've ever mentioned that Big Ears' mom is cool. I bet I've told you because I always say it whenever I get the chance, and I usually think it even more. She's cool on the inside and cool on the outside. What I mean to say is that she's pretty and nice. One day she stroked my hair the same way she did on report card day, and I dreamed later that night that I was older and that I married her. It was a happy dream until Big Ears' mom said, "Honey, I want you to meet your stepson."

And she pointed to Big Ears. When I woke up my heart was beating really fast. I'm not surprised. You gotta be really patient to have Big Ears as a friend, but you have to be really brave to have him as a stepson, and I'm a coward, I admit. I couldn't take it. After that I gave up on the idea forever of marrying Big Ears' mom. I'm not sure what is more of an issue, the age difference or Big Ears himself.

There we were, on the bench in the hallway. We were still waiting in line for the butcher. Ozzy and his grandpa had just come out. Ozzy started screaming like a madman, "I only failed four subjects and passed three! Manolito,"— he grabbed my shoulder and shook me—"I passed three: gym, religion, and shop! Grandpa, you know how tough religion is; you want me to tell you the nine commandments?"

"No, buddy, don't tell me any commandments," his grandpa answered, and then he whispered to my grandpa, "He's a brute, but at least he's optimistic."

Ozzy's grandpa had to calm Ozzy down because he had gotten a little out of control with all the excitement. He had started walking on his hands, and then he had lost his balance and landed on the One-and-Only Susana's grandma.

"Every once in a while, this guy needs a little calming

down. It's just what the doctor ordered."

But this particular time, Ozzy needed a lot of calming down because he had started doing cartwheels to show the audience why he had gotten an A in gym.

"I better get him out of here before something bad happens," said Ozzy's grandpa.

Everybody thanked him, and Susana's grandma sighed and said, "It was about time. Now we can finally relax."

Susana's grandma doesn't know that Ozzy is her granddaughter's boyfriend, or at least, one of the thousand of boyfriends Susana has.

After a little while, it was Paquito Medina's turn. He went into the classroom and came out right away with his report card. He folded it and put it in his pocket, and then he said to me, "Manolito, you wanna go to Hangman's Park this afternoon?"

I nodded, even though I knew I wasn't going to be allowed to go out that afternoon. Miss Asunción came out for a second to tell Paquito Medina, "Make sure to call your mom to tell her the good news."

Then, Paquito Medina got super red and ran away without saying a word.

Susana's grandma had fallen asleep. She had her mouth open and was going: "Zzzzzzzzzzzzz."

When it was the One-and-Only Susana's turn, my grandpa went to shake her grandma to wake her up, but Susana said, "No, no, let me. I know what to do." Susana got close to her grandma's ear and said real loud, so we could all hear, "Grammy, the soap opera's about to start."

As if she had been wound up, Susana's grandma closed her mouth, opened her eyes, and put on her glasses, which she wears around her neck on a little chain.

"Doesn't she do it in record time?" asked Susana.

When her grandma looked around and saw us all, it seemed like she didn't know where she was. She opened and closed her eyes a few times, and then she got up to go in to see Miss Asunción. She came out half protesting: "I don't understand the grades they use these days. My daughter tells me to come with Susi, and I say, 'What for, if I don't even understand them?'"

And Our Teach said, "Basically, she passed, but she's got to improve her behavior. She's a little hooligan."

And Susana, taking advantage of the fact that Miss Asunción wasn't looking, stuck out her tongue.

Everything around me was getting a little hazy, like a dream you want to wake up from as soon as possible. When my name was called—Manolito García Moreno—I don't know what happened, but my legs started shaking.

My grandpa and I went over to Miss Asunción's desk.

"Well, Manolito, you know what you got, right?"

She looked at me over the top of her reading glasses. I swallowed hard and said, "Yes, Miss Asunción."

Then she turned to my grandpa and said, "Math, like always. I hope you're going to give him a little extra push this summer. He's not one bit stupid, but he gets easily distracted, and talks nonstop, and he gets together with that

López, who doesn't know his left ear from his right, and with Ozzy, who's a potential delinquent . . . and here are the results: then I have to give him an F. They don't call it an F anymore, but you and I know what it is; he failed and that's all there is to it. He's lazy, very lazy. When he wants to, and he applies himself, he passes, but this time he just didn't feel like it."

I was looking at the ground, so the tear that came out of my left eye hit the left lens of my glasses and got it wet, and all of a sudden I was a one-eyed kid.

"And tell his mother not to get hysterical, because I know her. So she feels better, you can tell her that his friends are even worse off than he is," said Our Teach.

"Yeah, but they don't care,"—my voice was all shaky—"and I do."

"If you care so much, why didn't you study?" asked Miss Asunción.

"Because I don't like math," I said. Another tear came out of my right eye. It looked like my shoes were in a puddle.

My grandpa took out his handkerchief from his pocket and wiped off my runny nose, my tears, and my glasses.

"This summer we're going to study every afternoon, and he's going to get an A next year," he said to Miss Asunción.

"I'm sure of it," answered Miss Asunción. "If he applies himself, he can do it."

The way home seemed shorter than usual. My grandpa was telling me about great scientists, writers, and inventors who had failed math.

"Cervantes, Einstein, Fleming, Jules Verne . . . They all had something in common: they all failed math."

"And what did their moms say?"

"Well, they got over it, Manolito. They got over it."

We were in front of Stumbles. Mr. Ezequiel was at the door and he asked, "What's wrong, Manolito?"

"The little guy failed math," answered my grandpa, "and I've told him that it's not the end of the world."

"Does your mom know?" asked Mr. Ezequiel.

I shook my head and Mr. Ezequiel sighed. "Poor Manolito, come have a Coke before you go up."

I felt like crying. I shook my head again, and I headed toward home. My grandpa stayed at Stumbles. I can't blame him, because they already had poured his glass of

red wine, and when my grandpa sees a glass of red wine, he can't resist it. It's like a magnet, and this supernatural force pulls him toward it, and even if he doesn't want to, he has to drink it. I'm serious. One day he explained it to me and my grandpa doesn't lie.

I started to go up the stairs to my apartment. When I got to the floor where Our Nosy Neighbor Luisa lives, she opened the door right away.

"I was cleaning the peephole and I saw you."

Luisa cleans the peephole several times a day. My mom says that Luisa remembers to clean the peephole every time she hears someone going up or coming down the stairs.

"What's the matter, Manolito?"

"I got my report card, and I passed almost everything."

"And which subject didn't you pass?"

"Uh . . . math."

"And does your mom know?"

"Well, no," I said, but she was going to know in a couple of minutes.

"Poor Manolito," Luisa said to me, and I cried on her bathrobe for a while. "If she starts screaming, get three changes of clothes out of the closet and run away to my apartment, and I will give you a bed and food and a private tutor that your godfather will pay for."

I blew my nose in her handkerchief, and before she went back into her apartment she looked at me and said, "Man, you're really upset. You should see what just came out of that little nose of yours."

I only had ten more steps to go before I got to my apartment. I went up three and sat down. Now there were only seven left (and they say I stink at math).

I thought that nothing could save me from my mom's lecture. I opened my report card and looked at my F one more time. I wished I could change that lethal grade. There was no way, though. My mom can't be fooled that easy. My dad calls her Detective because when he comes home from a trip she examines him from head to toe, behind his ears and around his neck, to make sure he has showered every day like she tells him.

A long while went by. My grandpa came up the stairs real slow. Judging by his speed, I guessed he had . . . three glasses of wine (and they say I'm not good at doing math in my head).

"Manolito, you're still here?"

"I was scared to go in alone."

The two of us went in together. My mom put out her hand and said, "Let's see what you got, Manolito."

The Bozo was eating. He was having soup and it was dripping down his mouth, and he was breathing like he had a cold, like a little pig. I sat down next to him. My mom closed the report card and said, all mad, "I knew it; I knew it. There goes our summer! We're going to have to stay here without going anywhere all because of this lazy boy."

"We weren't going to go anywhere anyway, Catalina.

We don't have any money to go on vacation," said my grandpa.

"Dad, you be quiet. Before you go putting your foot in your mouth, you be quiet. He thinks only about playing, hanging around outside, being a little hoodlum, and about upsetting his mother, like he is right now. He doesn't care at all about upsetting me."

I started crying again and getting my glasses all wet. The Bozo saw me and wanted to give me a spoonful of his soup, but when he saw I didn't want any, he started crying, too. When I start crying, he starts crying. That's how it always is.

"Now the other one's crying," my mom said, sitting down on the couch. "You're all out to get me."

"Catalina, it's not a big deal. So what, the little guy failed math? He'll make it up next year! A lot of important men" (I always wonder how my grandpa knows so much about the history of humanity) "failed math when they were little: Cervantes, Shakespeare, Edison—"

"Stop with the speech about great men who failed math," my mom cut him off. "Besides, what do *you* know, Dad?"

"I know that what you need to do is help the little bugger get an A next year and that chewing him out isn't the way to do that."

"Oh, yeah?"

"Yeah, and you should know it, too, since you failed math two years in a row."

Man, that was a low blow. The Bozo and I stopped crying immediately. There was a classic deadly silence, and the Bozo sat there looking at my mom. I never would have suspected that about my own mother. It was a big letdown. I had been idealizing her. You think the Bozo doesn't understand, but he's a quick little fellow.

"I don't think it's appropriate for you to be telling him that. . . ." My mom was a little speechless.

"Why not?" my grandpa asked. "Your son should know that a woman as smart as his mom, a woman who surprises us every day with her intelligence, also failed math."

"But, Dad, I took it again the next year and passed," she said apologetically.

"Manolito's going to do the same thing. Next year he's going to take it again and surprise us all. Right, buddy?"

Warning: in my home we're all a bunch of cry babies. I had to dry my tears on the Bozo's bib, wipe my nose with my mom's handkerchief, and my mom wiped her tears on my grandpa's handkerchief, and my grandpa wiped the Bozo's nose, and the Bozo dried his tears with my mom's hand, and that's not even the half of it. We're experts at these kinds of scenes.

During lunch that day, we ended up wiping our noses and tears on the tablecloth, and we made big plans for the summer: in the morning we'd go to the pool with my grandpa and in the afternoon I'd study math. Well, it's not like it was this great plan, but the moment of the lectures had passed.

Night came. It was my first night after my first F, so I couldn't sleep.

"Grandpa, is it true that Mom failed math two years in a row?"

"No, it's not true; she failed it three years in a row."

Three years! No way!

"But she was lucky because you were her dad and you never chewed her out," I said.

"Who told you I didn't chew her out?" asked my grandpa.

"You never chew *me* out."

"Because I'm your grandpa."

"My supergrandpa," I corrected him.

But there was something else, something that was bothering me:

"Grandpa, we still have to tell my dad about the F when he comes home on Friday. What do you think he'll say?"

"Give me my dentures. I can't give a long explanation without my dentures." Once he put them in, he chomped down in order to snap them into place and he kept talking. "I have come to an agreement with your mother, but we both have to hold up our end of it: you and me. You're going to study this summer, and we won't say anything to your dad about the F. We'll tell him next year, once you've gotten your grades up."

"And my dad won't be mad that we lied?"

"We'll tell him it wasn't a rotten lie, but a little white lie. On top of it, your dad never gets too mad. All right, here, take my dentures. Put 'em back in the glass."

The dentures fell down into the glass, and some powder came flying up. The glass looked like one of those globes that have snowmen and snow in them.

"Grandpa, am I just going to study all day long?"

"Manolito, the summer is very long. You'll be able to study, go to the pool, go to Hangman's Park, have an ice cream at Stumbles, watch movies on TV, spend time with Big Ears and with Paquito Medina, fight with Ozzy, count your toes, and get bored from not doing anything. No F could ever ruin your months of freedom when you don't have to go near school. . . ."

Or near Aunt Melitona, I thought.

We had the window open. Like every night in the summer, we could hear the people who were sitting at the tables outside of Stumbles.

I was embarrassed to tell my grandpa what I wanted to say to him, and what I wanted to say was . . .

"Grandpa, thank you. What would I do without you?"

I thought he was going to give me a kiss or shed a tear from uncontrollable emotion, but he didn't do any of that. I sat up to look at his face, and I saw his lips were sunken. They were sinking in more and more, and when he looked like a monster who was going to swallow his own face, he let the air out again and it blew my hair back. It was the classic sleep sigh.

I was so pumped that he hadn't heard what I said because even if it were true, in all honesty, it was not a statement worthy of a member of the Filthy Feet. All my friends would have laughed at me. But now, since no one could hear me, I could say things that my buddies wouldn't let me say in real life. Taking advantage of the fact that my grandpa was out, I said to him again, "Thanks, Superprostate."

I stayed awake for an extra-long while, listening to the laughter of the people down at Stumbles. The sounds of summer were cool. That was the first night of the first F of my life (I don't know why, but I had a feeling it wouldn't be the last), the first night of the first little white lie I told my dad (I had told a few white lies in my day already), and the first night of the longest summer of my existence because I still hadn't used up a single one of its days.

Summer was like a perfect ice-cream cone you admire for a moment before taking the first lick.

THE END

Look for more adventures of
Manolito Four-Eyes and his family
and friends coming to bookstores
in Spring 2010.